RUNNING BEFORE THAT WIND

RUNNING BEFORE THAT WIND

NEIL THOMPSON

Matador
5 Weir Road
Kibworth Beauchamp
Leicester LE8 0LQ, UK
Tel: (+44) 116 279 2299
Fax: (+44) 116 279 2277
Email: books@troubador.co.uk
Web: www.troubador.co.uk/matador

ISBN 978 1848764 873

British Library Cataloguing in Publication Data.
A catalogue record for this book is available from the British Library.

Typeset in 12pt Bembo by Troubador Publishing Ltd, Leicester, UK
Printed and bound in Great Britain by TJI Digital, Padstow, Cornwall

Matador is an imprint of Troubador Publishing Ltd

To My Daughter Robyn
and
My writing companions
Churchill and Rhys
Unto the pure all things are pure

ACKNOWLEDGEMENTS

David Grubb – for his support, advice and approval.

Andrew Morrison – for his encouragement and artwork.

Running Before That Wind is a work of fiction. The chapters are however based on factual situations which I have either personally experienced or observed in others. Some events, places and dates may have been altered in order to achieve continuity.

MAP OF SUDAN

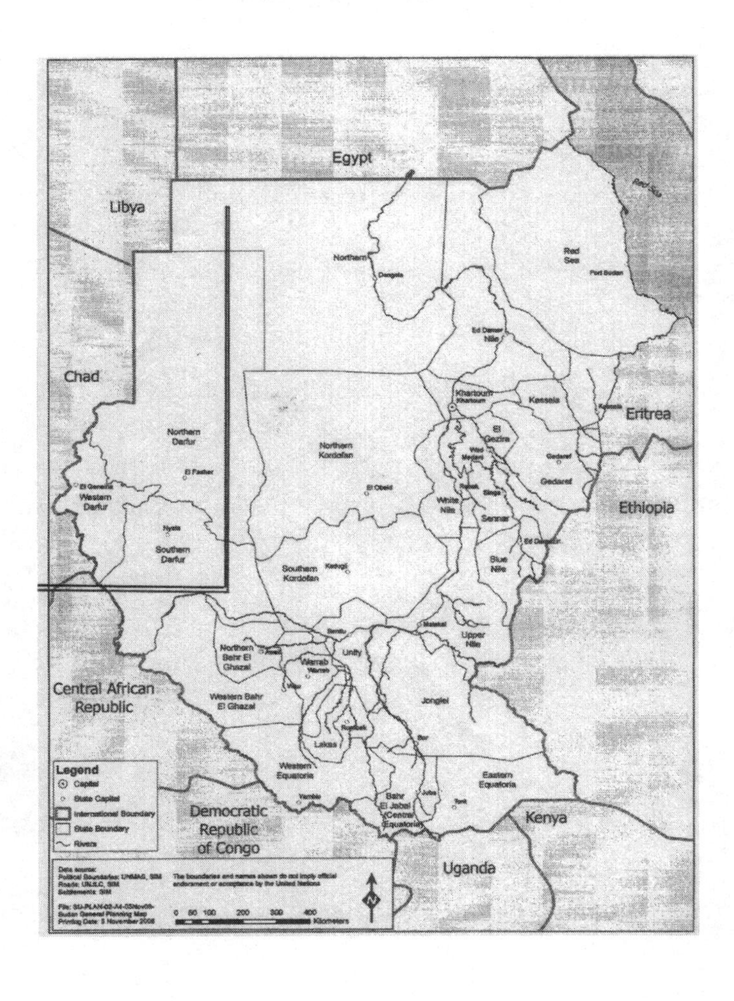

Egypt
Libya
Chad
Eritrea
Ethiopia
Central African Republic
Democratic Republic of Congo
Uganda
Kenya
Northern
Red Sea
Northern Darfur
Western Darfur
Southern Darfur
Northern Kordofan
Southern Kordofan
Khartoum
Kassala
El Gezira
Gedaref
White Nile
Sennar
Blue Nile
Upper Nile
Unity
Warrab
Northern Bahr El Ghazal
Western Bahr El Ghazal
Lakes
Jonglei
Western Equatoria
Bahr El Jabal (Central Equatoria)
Eastern Equatoria
Legend
Capital
State Capital
International Boundary
State Boundary
Rivers
0 50 100 200 300 400
Kilometers

MAP OF NAMIBIA

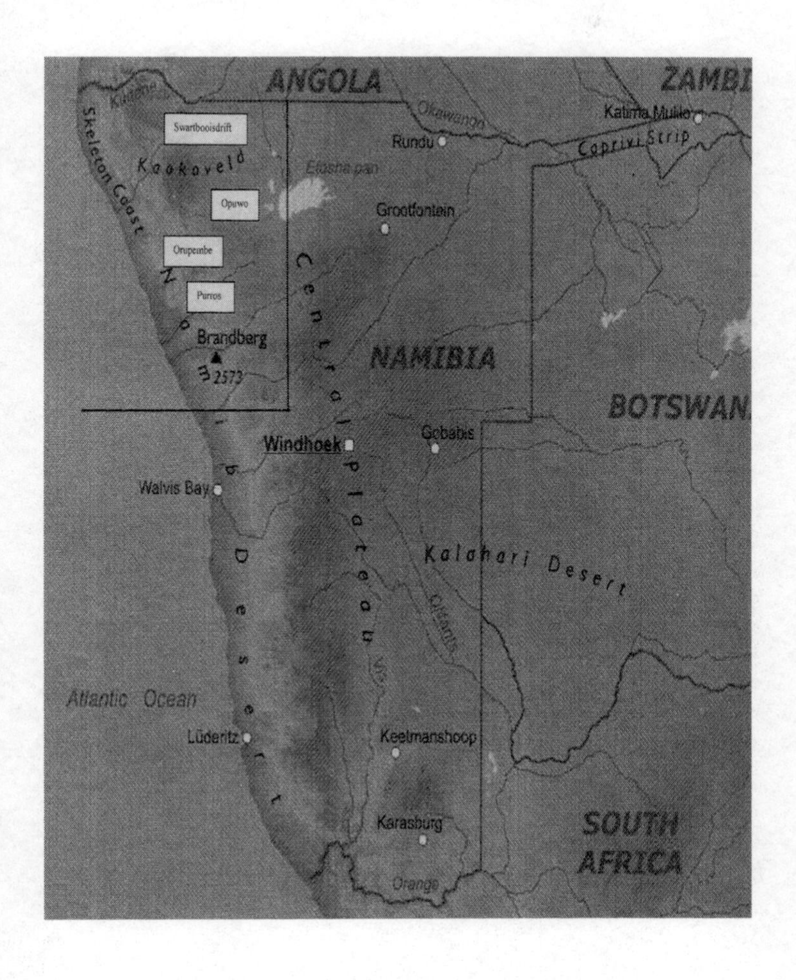

CONTENTS

Glossary xiii

Farmers Son 3

San (Bushman) 10

Finding the Silent Children 15

Running Before That Wind 31

Athlete 139

Physicist 149

Rock Climber 158

Ministers Wife 166

Teacher 175

Fleeting Touch 187

Expiation 197

Piano Tuner 208

GLOSSARY

Afrikaner - an Afrikaans speaking white person in South Africa
Afrikaans - an official language of South Africa
Baas - supervisor, sir (Afrikaans)
Baksheesh - a bribe, or tip (money)
Basie - little sir (affectionate)
Bedu - nomadic Arab of the desert – also known as the Bedouin
Black wildebeest - another term for gnu (Connochaetes gnou)
Bontebok - an antelope found in eastern South Africa (Damaliscus dorcas dorcas)
Dogwood - a tree with red stems and hard wood
Eastern Province - province in South Africa
Eland - the largest of the antelopes (Taurotragus oryx)
Gemsbok - large antelope (Oryx gazella)
Herero - people, tribe mainly from Namibia
Himba - people, tribe mainly from Namibia
Hottentots - refers to the Khoikhoi peoples
iKung - one of the Bushman tribes
Indaba - discussion, conference (South African)
Janjaweed - government milita group in Sudan, proven perpetrators of genocide
Kaokoland/veld - vast area, Kunene Region, Northern Namibia

Kaptein - captain, (sir)
Kaross - blanket made of skins
Khoisan - collective term for San and Khoikhoi peoples of Southern Africa
Kunene River - the river on north/western border dividing Namibia and Angola
'Kaptein, daar is iets baie verkeerd' - 'captain, there is something very wrong'
Lobola - a bride price, traditionally paid with cattle
Luister - listen (Afrikaans)
Lynx (Caracal) - Felis caracal
Magog - like cannabis, marijuana
Masalit - tribe living in central/western Darfur, Sudan
Meme - 'respected mother', Ovambo language, Northern Namibia
Missie - Miss, Little Miss (affectionate)
Nationalist Party - ruling political party during the 'apartheid years' in South Africa
Nkosi Sikele Afrika - National anthem of South Africa – 'Lord Bless Africa'
Oubaas - sir or 'old master' (affectionate – Afrikaans)
Plettenberg Bay - town/area, Eastern Province, South Africa
Port Elizabeth - town, Eastern province, South Africa
San - Bushmen group – Southern Africa
Skeleton Coast - north-western coast of Namibia
Sotho - group of people living mainly in Botswana, Lesotho and South Africa
SWAPO - South West Africa People's Organisation
Swartbooisdrift - tiny settlement on Kunene River
Trinidad - town in Cuba
Tswana - people, tribe in Southern Africa

Veld -open, uncultivated country in Southern Africa
Xhosa - people, tribe in South Africa
Zaghawa - nomadic tribe living in northern Darfur, Sudan
Zulu - people, tribe in South Africa

PART 1

The funeral was held yesterday.

Now as I sat in the twilight, in my fathers study, it was time to sort through his papers; keeping the important, setting aside any accounts still to be paid, discarding the rest.

It was not an easy thing to do. His writing, the small mementos, a paper knife, his diary, kept on bringing him back to me; it was all I could do not to weep for him, let alone try to go through his possessions. His faint clean smell, the subtle aftershave ever present.

He had always been a hoarder and a scribbler. Jotting down reminder notes, lists of birds and animals seen on his travels, Christmas and birthday cards stacked in shoe boxes. Slowly, sadly lethargic I went on. In the bottom drawer of his old desk were four dog-eared manuscript books.

'What have I found?' Out loud to myself. 'Never seen these before.'

Pausing, I almost didn't want to open them. Something wilful made me page through the first one. Then I was absorbed totally. Switching the desk light on, I saw that he had written what at first appeared to be short stories. It soon became clear that these were episodes from his life. Some anecdotes I knew of, others filled gaps in his younger years.

The years before he met my mother…

FARMER'S SON

Jim is an old friend of mine. We go a long way back to our junior school days in Canada. The scion in a wealthy, long established family, Jim had never really worked hard in his life. Big, bluff and good-humoured, he loved the outdoors; a practical, decent man with no airs and graces.

Inseparable as boys, we were in the same class at school, played football together, explored the forests around Vancouver and have always been close.

He was hunting in South Africa when he met Margaret, who was called Marge by all, a name she also insisted on. A feisty farmer's daughter brought up in the Sonora desert, down near Yuma in Arizona, she was a good looking blonde woman in a handsome, sunburnt way. Being an expert horsewoman, her legs were strong, large buttocks, muscular and firm.

To the surprise of many they married, settling on a large fifteen thousand hectare ranch in Namibia. They both loved Namibia; for its openness, pristine beauty and clean air. The contrasts of landscape and scenery; deserts, forests, savannah and scrub in a splendour untamed to the eye. They live there to this day and will never leave.

Shortly after they moved there, I went to visit them, taking the long flight from Vancouver to London, from

London to Windhoek. The first time they met me at the airport, but in the years that followed I would make my own way to their farm, a six hour journey by road. Being a keen birdwatcher and especially fond of raptors, I spent many contented hours walking around their property. Any unusual sightings would be recorded in a little notebook; date, time and place carefully annotated. Sometimes Samuel, an old coloured man of Bushman origin, would accompany me. After a lifetime in the bush, he could imitate the bird sounds, attracting the birds toward him with his calls.

Pursing his lips to issue a harsh 'tic-tic-chaa-chaa.' And a paradise flycatcher would scurry around the leafier thorn bushes repeating the sound. Or he would whistle. Coming back to him from a dry branch the scarlet chested sunbird would counter 'cheeup, chup, toop, toop, toop'.

I saw more with him than I ever would have alone.

Every year I visited them, it became an annual pilgrimic holiday. The first five years saw the birth of their two sons, substantial improvements made to the buildings and a steady change in farming practices. Fences were removed and the paddocks opened up. Jim cut back the encroaching bush, reduced the cattle herd, slowly re-introduced game and now was talking of trying to buy the farm next door.

This all seemed in total contrast to some of their neighbours. Inherited farms in the main; overstocked, devoid of grass, with owners who little appreciated what they now possessed.

It was at this time they acquired the leopard. Samuel had found it near a rocky outcrop about a kilometre from the farmhouse. Being tiny, almost newborn, he claimed that it had been abandoned. Neither the mother nor any other cubs could be found. Some initial confusion also arose, because to him both cheetah and leopard were called luiperd, the Afrikaans for leopard. Samuel, unintentionally, led Jim and Marge to believe that it was a cheetah, a far more gentle creature.

In fact, Samuel named it Xui, a Bushman Xko name meaning leopard; a name given fruitlessly however, as it never ever responded to being called.

But the Afrikaner neighbour put them wise. Marge decided to keep it anyway and raise it as a pet. This worried me. Expressing my concern to Marge during a visit, she listened carefully saying, 'I want to let it grow before trying to release it back into the wild.'

'Why don't you take it to a sanctuary?' I urged, 'they will know how to rear it.'

But she remained dogmatically steadfast.

When next I visited it was nearly two years old. The leopard had grown quickly, a solitary, difficult animal with a mind and nature of its own. There was no softness or timidity about this cat; its eyes were glaring and baleful. But it did seem to be sullenly domesticated. Nevertheless everyone gave Xui a wide berth except Jim and Marge and their two sons. To me it was clear that the animal was maturing, needed to hunt, would soon look for a mate.

Mentioning this to Marge, she replied, 'the local veterinarian is helping us to re-introduce it back to the veld. He seems to know what he is doing.'

The day had been a scorcher; the early evening was still very warm. Jim had taken the two boys back to boarding school, a journey of some six hundred kilometres. He was due back later the next day after getting them settled.

Marge and I sat at the poolside, talking, having a light cold supper and sharing a bottle of wine. An emotional sexual tension was growing between us, something that had never happened before. We chatted and laughed, she would touch my arm or leg. We swopped stories about the more eccentric people we knew.

Thirty kilometres away lived a burly German speaking farmer, Kurt Alpers. Whilst patrolling his farm he apprehended two poachers, who, at the time, were slaughtering one of his large Brahman cows. Not content with beating them up in retribution, Kurt and his son then forced each villain into a two hundred litre drum. Welding the lids closed, they delivered the drums to the local police station. Barely alive, the poachers were set free; charges now levelled in reverse against Alpers.

'What a cruel, barbaric thing to do,' I stated.

'You must remember,' Marge said softly, 'many of the white people here have struggled too. Some were incarcerated during the second World War, in appalling cells out in the desert. Others have suffered with droughts or lost their sons in the fruitless border wars. A direct retribution and quick punishment seems almost normal to them.'

I couldn't really agree but relaxed again and we returned to our easy-going conversation.

Then for a while we were quiet, sipping our wine and listening to the night-sounds; little scurries and calls, difficult to identify.

And then she said that she was going to swim. Slowly, in front of me, she stripped naked, smiled, turned and dived into the pool. I was instantly erect, aroused more quickly than ever before in my life. She beckoned. Shedding my clothes, I was soon in the water after her. We grappled, embraced, kissed; she was all over me, I was all over her. We barely made it to my bedroom, before I was in her and coming. Throughout that hot night, we made love, she constantly wet and aroused, crying out in enjoyment as her orgasms overtook her. As dawn broke the next morning, we were sitting facing each other, she in my lap, my penis deep inside her, her buttocks the only movement, clenching and releasing, clenching and releasing. Our arms bound around each other, her engorged nipples tight up to my chest; with her lips just touching mine, she whispered, 'Robert, you've been wonderful, you are wonderful, but we can never do this again. It's too addictive, in the end it will destroy all of us.'

'Promise me, please promise me.'

★★★

Adam, their third son was born later that year and this helped keep our attraction in check. Over the next few years our friendship was as strong as it had always been. The mutual trust based on the memory of that night would always be with us, the remembered desire and our physical well being, the lust and the love. The secret held.

Adam was unlike his brothers, not quite as robust and physical, not quite as loud. I observed him carefully, his colouring also seemed slightly different, the shape of his jaw and nose. His hands were finer, long fingers. I could see his mother in him, but saw more of myself in him than Jim.

But Marge said nothing; and Jim was happy, he adored the boy. With the two older ones away at boarding school, little Adam became his favourite.

★★★

I was in London on a week's vacation, when the telephone rang in my bedroom.

'Robert, oh thank goodness I've got hold of you.' It was Marge, her voice quivery, as if she was close to tears.

'How did you find me?'

'I phoned your practice, the receptionist gave me your number.'

'Please Robert, you must come and help us. Adam is missing. Everybody is looking for him, the neighbours, people from town. Jim is out of his mind!'

'Is Old Samuel there?' I asked.

'No, he's in the Kalahari, visiting family,' she replied.

Her despair overwhelmed me for the moment, my heart seemed to stop. I sensed, knew, why she had called.

'You are our closest friend. You know this farm as well as anybody.'

It was a fraught afternoon. I cancelled a pre-arranged dinner with an elderly aunt, managed to secure a flight booking and rushed out to Heathrow. In between, there were telephone calls to and from my receptionist; appointments re-scheduled, finding locums to stand in during my extended leave of absence.

I had been fortunate to get a flight that night, arriving

at Windhoek airport early the next morning. She met me at the airport. As I hugged her, she pulled me close, her mouth to my ear. 'You know, don't you. Tell me you know,' she sobbed.

'I know, Marge, I've always really known.'

As we drove northwards she sat close to me, holding my hand in hers. She, trying to draw some comfort from my presence, the anguish and suffering etched on her face, was also inscribed in our hearts.

I was alone when I found him the next day. What remained of him. There is a large old camelthorn tree, a special place where I often watch a large martial eagle. Adam's small, mutilated body was at the top of it, wedged in a vee of the highest bough.

The leopard Xui was never seen again. He had returned to the wild.

★★★

SAN (BUSHMAN)

Over the years I have met many people, people of varying temperaments, religious persuasions and race groups.

My interest has always been to find someone who is totally happy and contented; a person comfortable with himself; settled in his surroundings, and always of the same good demeanour.

Amongst the wealthy I have never found it. The gratification of acquisition is too strong. Middle class endeavours to acquire. The poor, often under-educated, struggle to break the shackles of squalor and alcohol. Those who claim happiness in religion are almost always affected by dogma.

Samuel, an iKung Bushman, a cattle herder, illiterate yet wise, who lived on Jim and Marge's farm in Namibia, is the only person I know totally at peace in his environment. He could engender peace around him too.

A sedate influence came over cattle when he herded them. A quiet call, a slightly discordant low whistle; the animals would walk back to the kraal in steady response. At dipping or inoculation time, there would be no bellowing or rampaging around. Samuel's affinity kept them calm.

'Come, my gentle beings, my king and queens,' he would sing, tapping them indulgently into order with a long pliant stick. A fractious cow disrupting the herd, or a sickly calf, would be separated out with the minimum of fuss and effort.

With the San, beauty, handsomeness, is a fleeting thing. The elastic skin tissue breaks up quickly. Sun and wind, harsh outdoor living, makes these small people, as adults, look older than they are.

'How old are you, when were you born?' I once asked him.

'I was born when men went across the big water to fight,' he replied, referring to the Second World War. He must have been in his fifties when I first got to know him.

Surprisingly, Samuel had also seen military service. During the 1970s the Bushman battalion had been an integral part of the South African Defence Force; based in the Caprivi strip during the border confrontation with SWAPO, Angola and the Angolans' furtive Cuban mercenaries.

From his commanding officer, an English speaking captain, he learnt a fair amount of English. Into this, he interspersed an astonishing array of descriptive clicks and sounds.

When Marge, an American and Jim, a Canadian, settled in Namibia, they were referred to Samuel through a Non-Government Organisation working in Bushmanland. At the time he was no longer in the army. Marge and Jim asked him to work for them. English speakers were scarce in the local populace.

'It is my land,' he said enigmatically, 'I will come.'

As they grew to know him, they realised what he meant. Their farm was in an area where Samuel's predecessors had moved to and from, probably for hundreds of years; hunting, food gathering, obtaining water. Trekking to it in the good times, away from it in the bad.

Their knowledge, their existence, sometimes in the harshest of terrains, made this their land.

Diaspora, irretrievable and irreparable, came to the Bushmen too.

As Jim improved the farm, removed fences and rotated grazing, Samuel would often comment, 'wild animals come back one day, small and big. Birds even more.'

Even though he had a room and could eat from Marge's kitchen, he still maintained his own lifestyle, living off veld food, tubers and melons. Occasionally he would hunt, killing a duiker or trapping a hare. Sometimes not eating for days. But when he had something, he would eat the lot. A traditional lifestyle of storing up bodily for the leaner times ahead.

Money was of no use to him. Every month Jim would pay him and every month Samuel would hand it back.

'Keep it for me, my baas,' he would say. 'When the rain no longer comes and the sun no longer shines for me, I will need it then.'

He slept outside with his animal skins as mattress and blankets.

I would go and sit with him sometimes, sharing his fire. Mostly he would talk.

'We only kill for food or in self defence. Never for size or horns.' Implying, but not saying it, and with a soft crinkly grin, the folly of trophy hunting.

'To kill an animal is for us to live. We respect and thank it.' And, 'animals were people once like ourselves, they should be protected.'

The San believe that when one dies, the Greater God will determine what wild animal you become. There are noble animals like Eland, Giraffe and Oryx, least noble are Jackal and Hyena. One's lifestyle will determine His judgement. Their most revered animal is the Eland.

'Eland is the creature of life and the rising sun.' And he would get up from the fire and do a shuffling solo dance in honour, clapping, and stamping his feet. 'Our bush girls ask the eland for blessing; blessing to have children. Strong, good children who will care for other children, and provide for the old people.'

***

He would tell his stories and play music on a little thumb piano called a dongo, or pluck his bow. The muted sounds floating away into the clear night sky.

Marge and Jim's sons revered him. He looked after them as if they were his own.

As little boys, before they were old enough for school, a lot of time was spent with Samuel. He would show them how to make string from leaf fibre, create snares with gum and insects to catch birds. And as he taught them bushcraft, he would play little practical jokes.

Samuel would cut three foot long reeds and show them how to push them into the sand river beds and drink. Sometimes he would plug the ends and smile at the boys futility. Or he would loosen an end of their bows when they were practising. Their arrows would wobble off in front of them. His giggling was infectious. It was always good humoured and kind.

The four of them would play riotous games of djani; flicking guinea fowl feathers in the air with flexible sinewed reeds. Seeing how long they could keep the play going. Samuel always made sure he lost.

★★★

The story of Adam's death carried deep into the Kalahari, where Samuel was visiting his family at the time. On his return, he did not need to be shown where the small body was found. He went there of his own accord. In front of the tree, he painted black and white stripes on his face. For a while he sat there, in the sand, studying the locality. It was getting quieter now. The birds settling for the night, cicada ceasing their noise. A coolness in the air as the sun sank below the horizon. Noiselessly he stood up; put his hand on a gash in the bark, a claw scratch.

It was a place he never went near again.

★★★

FINDING THE SILENT CHILDREN

My friend Chris has been to Darfur. Not in the normal way.

He was not in the ineffectual peace keeping force nor was he working for an aid agency. He was not a journalist, nor a government delegate.

Chris went to Darfur out of conscientious curiosity. It took him three months to get there and back. But for the two Bedu who accompanied him, it is almost certain that he would not have survived.

One reads about atrocities. Chris knew of Cambodia, had read about Rwanda and Kosovo. He had heard of the suffering in Angola, where some two million people are amputees, one in every four or five individuals. As Darfur featured evermore in the news, he was sparked to see for himself. His interest was galvanised into a covert action plan.

Knowing that I had spent a lot of time in Africa, he asked me to help him.

'Robert, I want to see if the news is exaggerated. See what the hell is going on.'

'But why?' I asked.

How do you explain the holocaust of a Darfur? The genocidal mass killing of indigenous peoples; black

Africans persecuted by lighter skinned Islamic Africans. Or is that the answer? The Islamists are not true Africans, have no deep roots, origins in Africa. They have allowed the Chinese to become their paymasters in return for the natural resources that belong to others, the black tribes that have always inhabited Darfur.

How do you explain the total destruction of tolerance and co-habitation? Millions of fleeing, starving, dying refugees without hope, without food, water, firewood. Resources depleted beyond replacement.

The environment, the land denuded.

'All my life I've heard of these events, starting as a young boy when Vietnam was on the go. Like so many people, I read about them and do nothing. Maybe to ease my conscience, I'll donate a few dollars. Much of which gets swallowed up by administration; the people who suffer the most get almost nothing.'

'You haven't answered my question,' I said.

He looked at me, with a determination on his face that I'd never seen before.

'Firstly, I want to see if what we hear or read about is true and if it is, to help at least one suffering person directly and properly.'

'That sounds a bit self serving, good for your ego only.'

'No..., if I can help one person, I will use that experience to help the next and so on. Maybe generate funds for a building project, a clinic or a small school. Use my construction skills in some way. I have a lot of leave due, there must be something that can be done!'

My voice was warning. 'The danger is immense, the risk enormous. If they catch you, the bandits, government militia forces, Chinese operators or even the refugees will kill you without a second thought. Like an irritating mosquito. You have no accreditation, no status, no publicity, just a nuisance getting in the way. You will have to be totally clandestine.'

'You're right,' Chris said, 'that's why I want you to help me. I don't expect you to go with me, just assist me with the planning. Start me in the right place, find local people to go with me, sort the paperwork out. I am going to Darfur, you have to get me back.'

I looked at him. Slightly overweight, a modest civil engineer who'd always been happy in his job, behind his desk, designing bridges, culverts and road structures.

'What about your family, what do they think?'

Sheepishly, quietly he replied, 'I haven't told them, didn't want to upset Pamela and the kids. I'm banking on you telling them, but only after I've gone out there.'

'You must be joking. You need to tell them,' I exploded.

'No, I can't. I know I need to, have even tried to, in a roundabout way, but it's been too difficult.'

Chris's voice was firm however; 'they may try and deter me, but I will not be put off from going.'

***

He had originally wanted to start from Khartoum, but I soon convinced him that he wouldn't get out of the airport building let alone obtain a visa.

I persuaded him to start in Cairo. 'I have a friend and colleague who might be able to help us.'

'But if we involve others, how can we keep it secret?'

'One thing an Egyptian understands, the right amount of money buys secrecy.'

Dr Akil Nasr, my dermatologist friend put us in touch with his younger brother Awan, a one man tour operator who did personalised trips to the Western Desert in Egypt. Chris's journey was planned, then underway.

We travelled by road from Cairo to Dahkla, a large oasis in the South West. There Awan loaded his Landcruiser. Supplies to last three months, water for longer, fuel to cover three thousand kilometres. Examining the vehicle carefully, I insisted on more spare parts. Another distributor and coil, an extra water pump, a host of seals, fanbelts and tubes. Every bolt was tightened, nipples and bearings thoroughly greased, all oils changed. Thorough preparation for deep desert travel.

The maps we obtained were old. Italian army maps going back to the 1930s, English explorers' maps even older. They were good enough. Nothing changes much in more than a million square kilometres of desert. There are no towns or villages, no settlements and no roads. Tracks are obliterated by wind and sand. But with the advent of GPS and satellite phones, a reliable map, no matter how dated, was more than sufficient.

In Dahkla another person joined the party, a Bedu guide named Munahid. A wiry tough-looking man who had grown up in the desert. His nomadic father still lived out there, moving his camels between Sudan, Libya and Egypt, as his fathers and forefathers had done for hundreds of years.

There were long, sometimes heated discussions

between Awan and Munahid that we could not understand, as our plan was outlined. The Bedu insisted that we remain in Dahkla for another week.

Awan explained, 'Munahid is contacting his father.'

'Where is he?' Chris asked.

'He lives amongst the Zaghawa, they are nomads like him,' Awan said, somewhat indifferently.

'Why?' It was my turn to question.

'To tell him where we are going,' he replied, a little enigmatically.

Chris whispered to me, 'Can I trust these people?'

'You are here now, what choice do you have? Akil Nasr says that you have paid the right money. Awan will not let you down.'

★★★

With a sense of some trepidation, I watched them leave the oasis. Hitching a lift back to Cairo with a group of geologists, I returned via London to Vancouver. Pamela, Chris's wife was aghast when I told her the news.

'Gone to Darfur!' she cried, 'I don't even know where it is.'

'It's an area between Sudan and Chad, one of the most dangerous places you can imagine, more than you can imagine,' I replied. 'Chris said that he'd tried to tell you.'

And then I told her what lay ahead for him.

'Chris said he was going to Egypt on some engineering business. Why could he not tell me the truth? He will never come back from that place. What does he think he's doing!' She went on, 'I've had a feeling that he's been hiding something. I've been so hurt; have buried myself at home and with the kids. What are we going to do now? And what about the children? How are they going to cope? He will die out there.'

How do you answer, explain to someone else's wife, the change that can come over one. How a conscience can lie dormant for just so long? How bravery and strength emerge in different ways. Or how a quiet, introspective person can take on the most dangerous journey, to satisfy that conscience.

★★★

From Dahkla they travelled southwards. Leaving the main road, they veered south-westerly heading toward Jebel Uweinat, following the early 20th century exploration routes of Clayton, Bagnold, the scholarly clever Egyptian Ahmed Hassanein and an intriguing Hungarian Almasy, known to the Bedu as Abu Ramla, "Father of the Dunes".

Through the desert they headed for the point where Egypt, Libya and Sudan meet. There is no border post or fence. One comes to a point on the map and then you are in Sudan. Three days after leaving Dahkla, they were camped near Ain Doua.

Their next point of reference was Jebel Jerhauda. They could see it in the distance, a huge, forbidding vague shape of mountain.

'We are lucky not to have seen anyone, but will have to be more careful. Not from the Sudanese yet. The

Libyans are more dangerous. They don't recognise the borders. They poach, killing the last few waddan. They believe this all belongs to them,' Awan told Chris.

'What is a waddan?' Chris asked.

'It is a sheep, big horned. I think you call it a Barbary,' Awan replied descriptively.

They drove more slowly now, southwards, trying to keep the travel dust to a minimum. Cooking was done on a kerosene stove, no chance was taken on making a fire. They packed everything away at night, slept on the ground right next to the vehicle. Ready to move on at the slightest inkling of danger.

Some mornings, before sunrise, Chris lay in his sleeping bag watching the eastern horizon gradually become lighter; the deserts' subtle sounds filtering around him. A fennec fox might call quietly; very occasionally sparrows and desert wheatears chirping, as they flitted around the camp site.

Sometimes, to his surprise in that aridity, where it had not rained for so many years, there would be a smell of moisture. A sweet fragrance of dew or rain. A vapour gone in a moment.

North Western Sudan is a desolate, barren area. The plains unending, followed by the dunes unending. Some three hundred kilometres into it, the Bedu told them to stop. He spoke quietly to Awan, who turned to Chris.

'See that camel skull, up the little wadi, to our left?'

Through his binoculars he could only just make it out, some eight hundred metres away. How the Bedu could see that with the naked eye was astonishing.

'We are going to camp there,' the Egyptian continued.

It was still early. Chris was surprised at their stopping, but said nothing. The day stretched into night and when he crept into his sleeping bag, he wondered what was going on. He thought he heard something, a noise, voices, but was weary, soon asleep.

It must have been just before dawn when he awoke. Chris sat up. On his haunches near Chris, looking on at him implacably, was an elderly man in Bedouin dress. Next to him Munahid, the guide, was talking softly. The look was not judgmental, just a test of the white man's resolve, of his determination. Then the old Arab looked away. Chris felt that something had been decided.

Awan moved into view.

'Who is this?' Chris asked.

'This is Marwan, Munahid's father,' Awan replied.

'What is he doing here? Where has he come from?'

'From Merga. This place, this desert is where he lives.'

Awan went on, 'Marwan and Munahid will take you further. I am turning back to Dakhla, to Egypt.'

'How will you get back?' Chris questioned.

'With the Landcruiser. You are going with the two Bedu, father and son, on foot.'

'But all our water. And food?'

'Marwan has his camels, they will carry everything, including you. Or you must walk. It will be too dangerous for me to stay with you. Even more so with a vehicle.'

★★★

Day after day they walked. The Bedu insisted that Chris wear a traditional robe with a head dress to protect him from the sun. Not being used to it, he found the headrope heavy and uncomfortable. But the white cotton garment surprised him; it reflected the sun's rays and was light and cool. He could also see that is was more than that; he looked like his companions. To an observer they were just three nomads plying the ancient trading routes of their predecessors.

The heat was relentless. They walked mostly from dusk to dawn. During the day they would rest. In the riverbeds, wadis, there were a few scraggy acacias and occasionally some shade. If the wind wasn't blowing they would rig up a small tarpaulin and shelter from the sun underneath it.

There was a period when the wind blew so strongly that their only protection were the animals. The Bedu showed Chris how to huddle up against a camel, shielded by its large body.

He lost weight. The walking, little food, the rigour took thirty kilograms off him in a month. His boots wore out. Marwan made up a pair of leather sandals for him to wear. The only liquid intake was water and copious quantities of mint tea. He was fitter and lighter than at any stage of his adult life.

But his brain was dormant. The slog, day after blistering day, sapped him mentally. Unless something unusual happened, his mind really only thought of one thing. Place one foot in front of the other.

In the immensity of the desert, Chris felt that he was no larger than a grain of sand. Just a tiny speck lost in a vast area. His only sustenance was to keep going.

They saw no-one, not a bird or animal. The land appeared devoid of life.

★★★

By his calculations, they had covered over six hundred kilometres; half the distance by vehicle, the rest mostly on foot. Occasionally he rode a camel, with one of the Bedu leading it. They were now going in a westerly direction, through northern Darfur, when the old man stopped. Without saying anything he pointed to left and right. Chris trained his binoculars; in the distance he could see a rocky cairn, further on another one.

The three men and their camels were now crossing into Chad. From his notes, Chris knew that the nearest refugee camp could be less than ninety kilometres away. The younger Bedu spoke, his broken limited English emphasising the situation, 'my father say, people nearby, we must be careful, quiet.'

'What people?' Chris asked.

'He not know who, just near.'

Marwan discovered them that night. It was a place only an Arab nomad would know. They were in a small inhospitable, rocky valley, sustained by a muddy patch, a tiny seepage of water which oozed to the surface. A group of five: four women, one heavily pregnant and a boy of about six. They were Masalit, jet black Sudanese people, ethnically terrorised. Systematically being wiped out by their Islamic leaders.

Their story of flight was harrowing. Munahid, who spoke a little Massa, translated.

'We were about twenty when the Janjaweed found us. Our men, fathers, brothers, sons were lined up next to each other, side by side, to watch. To watch as the Janjaweed raped us, each woman, even those pregnant, each raped by every soldier. The soldiers were more than fifteen.' The oldest woman held her fingers to indicate the count.

Even the hardened Bedouin were shaken.

'Proud men, Arabs, should not do this!' Marwan stated, fist raised in anger.

The woman went on, 'they murdered our men, one at a time, one bullet each, in the face. Some women were killed too.'

'What happened next?' Munahid asked.

'My sister, here,' the spokeswoman pointed to the emaciated woman next to her.

'When they were raping her, she cried to Allah for protection, for help, to save her.'

'And?'

'A Janjaweed took his knife to her, told her that she would never be permitted to speak again.'

Slowly she unwound the cloth that covered her sister's face.

The damage was horrifying.

Where her nose had been, there were now only two scabbed mucous-filled holes. She had no lips. Her teeth were totally exposed in a hideous, unremitting macabre smile. A mouth with teeth but no tongue. What remained of her ears were just small slivers of skin.

'What happened next?'

'The Janjaweed drove away in their trucks. We ran this way!'

'Food?' Chris questioned, barely audible, still shaken by the poor woman's face.

'Small birds, mice, even snakes,' came the reply.

'How can we ever help them?' he asked.

'We don't want anything from you,' the woman doing the talking said, 'only the plastic.' And she spoke behind her hand to Munahid.

'They just want plastic packets, you know like for shopping.'

'Why?' Chris asked.

The Bedu could not look up or at him when he replied. 'Their ....' he hesitated before he found the right word, '...genitals? were so damaged by the Janjaweed, they can no longer control their body functions. The women tie the plastic bags to hang between their legs catching the mess.'

Chris's mind swirled, he felt faint, sickened by what he had seen, made worse by the dreadful image of makeshift colostomy bags.

While Munahid made tea the three men conferred, pondering what to do next. Fate, or really nature, then intervened.

The pregnant woman went into labour. The instructions she gave were clear. If it was a girl, it should be saved, given a chance, if it was a boy it should be killed. Men had done her so much damage, there was no need for another one in this world. How, or in what manner, was not revealed. It was something she entrusted old Marwan with in private.

★★★

The return journey was exhausting beyond belief. The old man Marwan drove them on, keeping them going with stoic courage. A tensile strength tempered by the harshness of a desert lifestyle. He was kind and considerate in a concealed manner, always tending to his animals and companions before himself. Twice Chris collapsed, so weak, unable to walk. The thought of what they were trying to do, the stress of the situation, his exhaustion was as much mental as physical. The Bedu tied him carefully across a camel until he recovered his strength.

On the sixtieth day of their journey, through Sudan and eastern Chad and back, they reached Jebel Uweinat, camping in a small water course called Wadi Handal. From there, by satellite phone, Chris made two telephone calls. First, one to his wife, to tell her that he was safe. Chris was so emotional, could barely speak; Pamela immediately started to cry, as her love and relief spilled over. His second call was to me.

'Robert, I've made it! But now I need your help to get back home. Please meet me at Dakhla; cannot explain over the phone!'

My colleague, Dr Nasr was the facilitator. The authorities surprisingly understood. Baksheesh took place, papers were authorised.

***

Chris did what he said he would. The next mission is already being planned. Pamela, so openly proud of her husband, is now the mother of four children, two of her own and two of Sudanese origin. A boy of six and an eight-week-old baby girl.

A girl that the Bedouin had nurtured on diluted camel's milk during that terrible return journey. A girl whose mother was not only Masalit but part Zaghawa as well.

★★★

PART 2

I wished Dad had let me read them whilst he was still alive; the questions that he would have been able to answer. But I was also glad that he hadn't.

I stood stretched, went to the window, looked out at the night sky. The discovery of my father's early life was like that sky. The stars and lights illuminating; as was his writing; his words elucidating, lighting up his younger years.

Hanging on the opposite wall to his desk was his favourite painting, a landscape of open African space. He had tucked a photograph of my mother in the bottom left-hand corner. What joy the constant reminder must have brought him.

Sitting down again, I opened the next journal…

RUNNING BEFORE THAT WIND

It was at the large theatre in Vancouver where I met him.

As I settled down, a voice next to me asked if he could squeeze past as he had the next seat to my right.

The South African accent was instantly recognisable. We chatted whilst waiting for the performance to start and afterwards had a drink together in the bar downstairs.

It turned out that he was a single parent with his son just completing junior school, a school that was in the same neighbourhood as my home.

That first meeting has led to a life long friendship. A friendship that has stretched across continents and linked our two families.

★★★

'A Bushman dreams of his father's death'

I was sleeping next to the fire after a hunt and feasting, then dancing, when a dream came upon me and spoke to me.

The dream showed my father dead in the veld, in a sand riverbed, lying in the heat of the day.

And I was weeping and sad.

The dream was talking to me now, just as if it was my mother speaking. The dream was telling me of my father's death.

The wind was in the north and dust was covering the sky, as it does before the rains come. Many springbok passed by, followed by the other animals of the veld - gemsbok, eland and wildebeest. In my dream my mother said to me that it was the wind that was blowing them along; the animals were afraid. Were afraid of being caught by the wind and rain, afraid of being in the riverbed when the water flooded down.

So the dream told me of my father's death.

He had also been running before that wind

As the wind blew past, I felt my insides biting. I felt like that when one of my people died, my insides always ached when it was one of my people.
And now this was my father, whom the wind had overtaken.

(Bushman lore, many times told.)

May 2001

The landrover eased its way up the dune bank and out of the misty Kunene valley. The driver was always in wonder of the sight, as the early morning mist lay at a level with the top of the dunes and beyond that the clear desert sunlight took over.

Another magical and mystical morning. Cathan had experienced it so many times in the past and was always left in admiration and, at the same time, humbled. The colours somehow blended in; the light grey of the mist, the cerise of the dunes, the cloudless blue of the sky all linked together with the green trees in the water course and the pastel blues and purples of the mountains on the horizon.

***

He had spent the previous night at her grave. In the time-old African way, he had lit a fire which he fed steadily throughout the night. Sitting on an old canvas camp chair he told her of his plans for the future.

'Darling, I have to leave you now.' His throat constricted, choked, emotion weakening him.

'My contract is up. Our boy needs proper schooling. Your friend Felicity has written to say that Matthew can live with her. I think it's a good idea. Felicity will look after him in the best possible way.'

His voice tight, the sentences staccato.

'I'm not sure what I'll do. Perhaps work with Mom and Dad. See if they want me to help out or maybe even take over the running of the farm.'

'Bird is now getting very frail. He wants to live out his remaining days within his community and family.'

Pulling a blanket across his shoulders he spoke of the elephants, the kinship they as man and woman had found with them and how the herd was thriving.

'If my parents don't need me I may travel a bit. Experience new things, maybe travel a bit.You know I've always wanted to see the brown bears in Alaska, the blue whales of the ocean, the golden eagles in Scotland. Or study further, maybe lecture a little. Share my experiences with others, spend time with my family and our mutual friends, see how other people live and what their values are.'

Cathan was quiet for a while, looking deeply into the fire, trying to will her visage in the flickering flames.

He spoke to her of the many experiences they had shared, small and large.

'Do you remember how we met? And how you surprised me into marriage?'

He may have repeated himself and intertwined their shared experiences with his future plans, but never did he falter or grow tired. His sentiment ran high at times, with tears flowing down his cheeks. He continued to talk to her until the horizon in the east began to lighten.

'I love you, will always love you.'

'You enriched my life so much. I can't tell what you mean to me.'

'I will return here as often as I can. Bring our son here, you will always be remembered.'

Then bending forward he kissed the wooden cross that he and Bird had made that terrible day; tenderly touched the smaller one that stood next to it, and slowly left.

***

November 1988

Before commencing at College to do his Conservation Diploma, Cathan took leave of his parents and farm life for three months.

A house sitting vacancy arose in Plettenberg Bay: a wealthy retired doctor and his wife were on a world cruise. Cathan was left with a mansion on Millionaires' Mile to look after, supervising a full time housemaid and her older brother, the gardener, and caring for a boisterous labrador.

He despatched the maid back to her family.

'Don't worry, just come in once a week to dust and tidy up.'

The gardener was instructed to come in twice a week, with Cathan helping him in the grounds. It was an arrangement that suited all, the maid and gardener being paid even while not working. Cathan had peace and quiet; and the freedom to do as he wanted.

Within a few days he settled into an easy routine. Every morning he and the dog would run on the beach, plunging into the sea for a quick swim afterwards. Then on returning back to the house, he would tidy up and have breakfast. An hour or two would be spent in the garden, trimming and weeding edges. Then, if the weather was good, he would head back to the beach with either a surfboard or paddle ski, spending the remainder of the day in the sea and sun. On the occasional day when it rained, he would read and listen to music or take a drive into the surrounding area.

Every Tuesday and Thursday morning he worked with the old gardener. The grounds were large, the garden lush, with much for them to do. The old man, Joshua showed him how to propagate, cut and prune properly; lay out the flower beds. There was a greenhouse in a corner of the garden behind the house, where seedlings and bedding plants were grown; there were even some dubious looking plants of tomato appearance, which Cathan presumed was magog for the old man's private use.

They would work together and talk, with Joshua enquiring into Cathan's background and his aspirations for the future.

Politics, football and boxing would be discussed, with the old man displaying a wide knowledge of the pugilistic sport. He could recall fights and fighters going back many years and he knew the names of all the current world champions across the divisions. For a simple man, it was a prodigious memory.

'Flyweight Santos Laciar, undefeated nine world title fights.'

'Bantam weight Jeff Chandler from USA, probably the best in his division so far.'

'Eusebio Pedroza, what a featherweight, title holder for seven years, eighteen successful defences.'

'The welters, the division of many great boxers, Napoles, Cuevas, Hitman Hearns, Sugar Ray Leonard.

And then in the middleweights, that great fighter Marvellous Marvin Hagler, undefeated.'

'Nearly as good as Muhammad Ali, the best of all time!'

He told Cathan of the good black boxers around, how they struggled with little expertise to help them and facilities being virtually non-existent.

'There are boxers who are manipulated by promoters, take on fights when in poor condition or at short notice. Just to earn money to support large and extended families.'

And then there were the fighters who went down the crime route, working for the gang bosses; often succumbing to alcohol and drugs by the time they were thirty.

Politics was centred around the release of Nelson Mandela, who had already been in prison for more than twenty years. The old man was adamant that the Xhosa people would one day be the dominant tribe in government.

'Mr Mandela will be the first black president of a new South Africa. Black people will be able to vote and to own land and housing in white areas; schools will be open to all.'

Cathan listened quietly, asking, 'how will the minority groups be protected?'

To this the old man had no answer.

Twice a week they worked together, enjoying their companionship, discussions and arguments. The empathy they shared led both to a deeper understanding of elder and youth and, to Cathan, a greater understanding of the huge racial divide between the black and white peoples in Africa.

***

One early morning while out running on the beach, he stopped to look at a group of dolphins that were feeding and playing in the larger waves some fifty metres offshore. When Cathan turned around, he saw his dog far ahead, rapidly disappearing into the distance. Running after it he saw that the labrador was chasing another dog. Behind them in pursuit, someone else was also running along the beach. As he caught up, he saw that the figure was feminine, somewhat distraught, shouting to her dog to return. He went past her calling out, 'I'll collect my dog, hopefully yours will follow when I turn around.'

The labrador was apprehended and placed on a lead; her dog, a cocker spaniel, started to follow and he walked to where she was waiting for them.

'I apologise for my dog disrupting your walk,' Cathan said.

'No, it is my fault for not having a lead, just did not expect anyone else out this early,' she replied. 'Would you mind walking with me, then my dog will not take off again?'

Slowly they strolled back down the beach toward the houses. He guessed that she was in her mid-forties; an attractive woman with black hair framing deep blue eyes, tiny crows' feet on either side of each eye, a small snub nose and full lips surrounding a large mouth. Slightly overweight, she was wearing a black bikini top, which did little to conceal, and a pair of jogging shorts. There was a slight softness at the tops of her thighs and around her waist. Of medium height, her legs were shapely, with well-formed calves. She told him that she had arrived the night before.

'My husband and I have a small home on the inland facing side of Millionaires' Mile.'

He enquired about her family. 'No, we don't have any children,' was her reply, 'Jack is with a supporter's group for three months, following the England cricket team as it tours Australia. I am not very interested in cricket and have already been to Australia twice before. Plettenberg Bay, off season, in the early summer, is far more appealing.'

They parted shortly after. Cathan told her he ran every morning and offered to take her dog out for her. She smiled, 'I should also try and run every day as well, and with my dog on a lead so that it remains under control.'

★★★

Two days later, whilst waxing his surfboard before going into the sea, there was a quiet greeting behind him. Turning around, he saw her standing a few yards away; she appeared to have been there for a while, observing him prepare the board.

'Do you mind if I watch you? I know nothing about surfing. Is the sea not too cold at this time of the year?'

'It's cold,' he responded, 'but I surf in a wet suit and always come in when starting to feel hypothermic.'

They talked in generalities for a while and then he asked her if she would like to try.

She laughed. 'I don't know what to do, would fall straight off and make a complete fool of myself, and anyway the water is far too cold.'

Cathan suggested, 'you put the top half of the wet suit on, and I will wear the trouser section. If you sit on the surfboard, I'll push it out into the sea for about fifty metres, turn it around and then you can lie flat on the board and steer it across the smaller waves back to the beach. Try this a few times; you will soon get a sense of the board going over the waves. Once you have some confidence, I'll hold the surfboard in the water, show you how to stand on it, to position your feet correctly; then you could try and ride a few small waves.'

Leigh Ann was inwardly amused with herself. Lying on the warm beach afterward, she reflected on how much she had enjoyed the surfing, even as an absolute beginner. And whatever would her socialite friends in Johannesburg say if they had seen it!

She had managed to lie on the board and paddle through the waves out to sea. Gradually she went a bit further each time, but after an hour, following a call from Cathan she came back in. The tide was coming in. The waves were larger and more dangerous; it was time for a rest.

Cathan had gone out again and was riding the larger waves. His style was compact and strong. There were no tricks or flourishes, just an inherent grace and balance. Whilst she was watched him, he did not once fall off. He finished surfing and was now sitting next to her. To her surprise, a flask of tea had been produced and they shared a cup.

'Watch the sea', he pointed, 'see the way the current flows? Let's count the wave sets together, its almost certain that the sixth and seventh ones are largest.'

'Keep your eyes open for dolphins,' he also told her, 'as they often body surf through the waves close to shore and, being sociable, have no fear of humans and like to play. To get really close to them I use a paddle ski. If you want I'll bring it down for you one day and you can try and paddle on it.'

Leigh Ann was comfortable with him. Cathan had made no attempt to come on to her and kept his distance. Even when helping her on the surfboard, he had been careful where he put his hands and did not touch her. But lying in the sun, talking, being aware of him, she started to feel her interest growing. Whether it was the sun and sea, the exercise or his quiet voice in discussion with her, she could sense that her mood towards him was changing. With some amazement, she realised that she was sexually aroused, that her nipples were turgid and she was moistening between her legs. She could not believe herself; a forty-six-year-old woman whose hormones were kicking into overdrive like a teenager's.

They stayed awhile and through half closed eyelids she observed him.

She guessed that he was in his early twenties, but displaying a maturity beyond his years. She recalled that this was what had struck her when they first met. His demeanour was still, not calculating, more listening and considering; a small smile seemed to hover on his lips, as if all that he could see and hear was good. She could see that he was in fine physical condition with the long muscular thigh muscles of an athlete, a lean and hard upper body, strong arms and hands. Thick light brown hair, slightly bleached by the sun and a face that was good looking but without any distinguishing characteristics. His nose was slightly crooked, as if it had been broken at some time and never properly straightened. But it was his leonine eyes that astounded her; they seemed to change from brown to a dark golden colour, lighter in full sunlight, more brown when in shadow.

Her sexual tension eased as they continued to talk, he pointing out the birds and naming them for her, the cormorants, gulls, the different terns, tiny sanderlings and turnstones, offering little snippets of information on each, their migratory routes, nesting and feeding habits, their little quirks. She, who had never had any ornithological interest at all, was amazed at his depth of knowledge, and was fascinated, listening to his voice.

In contrast, Leigh Ann told him of the beaches she and her husband had been to: 'Bondi in Australia, the pebble beaches of Southern England, the beautiful unspoilt beaches of the Seychelles, and by accident the gay beaches on North America's West Coast. Everybody, I mean the men, clean shaven, all over, standing around like penguins. I looked.' And she giggled.

As they spoke, the distance between them seemed to become less and less, as if they were subconsciously inching closer together; even though they physically remained where they were. Their psyches were connecting. He was very aware of her, she was enthralled with him.

The afternoon cooled and they made their way home, he carrying the large surfboard under his right arm.

'I am expecting my mother to phone in from the farm this evening; looking forward to talking to her,' Cathan said.

They parted, thanking each other for a pleasant afternoon spent, and with a vague arrangement to meet again shortly, went their individual ways.

***

He had showered, put Van Morrison in the tape deck and was in the kitchen contemplating what to make for dinner, when the doorbell rang.

'I know it is a bit forward,' she said, looking somewhat nervous, 'but I've made a fish salad and have cheesecake for desert, if you would like to join me.'

She had two bowls in her right hand, each covered with a tea cloth and in her left hand there was a bottle of white wine.

They looked at each other; she at him with some trepidation; he at her with the knowledge that her life would be probably alter forever; that his would feel her influence for a long time.

'Your crossing the door's threshold may be a point of no return, for both of us,' he said softly, his eyes gentle, that small smile on his lips again.

He led her inside and while he set the table and

opened the wine, suggested that she pick a few flowers from the garden. These she arranged in a vase, placing it on the dining table between them. It was almost dark outside. With the windows and curtains open and the calm noise of the sea in the distance, they ate their dinner under dimmed lights.

Leigh Ann had dressed carefully, a pure cotton blouse, expensive brushed blue denims fitted tight, gold open toed sandals, a wide gold belt and fine necklace to match. She was beautiful in that light, her face glowing from the sun and from the feelings growing inside her; her hair, freshly washed and brushed through, was like gleaming ebony.

His eyes followed her every movement and gesture, he more openly admired her now and she felt free and happy, and light of heart. As they ate, they talked.

'Tell me of your parent's farm?' she asked.

'Well, it's more than our farm, it belongs to all.'

'I'm not sure I understand.'

'I'll tell you how it happened,' Cathan said.

One evening, nearly three years ago, as Cathan and his parents sat at the dining table after a meal, the land issue again came up. Black activism in the area was on the increase. More openly, pronouncements were being made that the white people would be driven from their farms and the land returned to the original occupants. This was a little hazy to the clearer thinking white residents, as the original occupants were Hottentots and Khoisan who were either subjugated, murdered or driven out by the Xhosa tribe. But the local Xhosa politicians now wanted retribution. Two white farmers in the vicinity had been killed and feelings ran high.

After debating the issue for a while, Cathan suggested to his father:

'we should turn our farm into a company, with fifty percent of the shareholding being retained by us. The balance can then be divided amongst each farmworker on a basis to be formulated on each person's individual length of service. A joint venture!'

He thought that an accounting firm which employed a black audit partner would be the best party to oversee the process. It should be an all or nothing approach, with all the assets being disclosed and valued.

Although his father had been thinking on these lines for some years, it was a more watered down version; a few acres of farm would be sold to each employee at a nominal value. But he trusted his son's views and two months later, Joseph Matanzima of the accounting firm Deloittes finalised the scheme. Joseph also agreed to help present it to the work force.

The presentation took place on two successive Saturdays. The first day was an indaba, the second devoted to making each individual understand the principles and documentation of the shareholding. During the afternoon prior to the indaba, a great fire was built, and a circle of logs for people to sit on was placed around it, an ox slaughtered, tea brewed. Half drums filled with ice and cool drinks were strategically placed between the logs which encircled the fire.

Before they started eating, his father addressed the gathering and thanked them for attending.

'You must all eat well for I have something very important to tell you when you are finished. I apologise for not having any bantu beer.'

And with a smile, he said, 'my wife does not have the correct recipe.'

It was a happy group that feasted that late afternoon. The smaller children running around and playing, and the women all seemed to be talking at the same time. The men were quieter, more circumspect. They conversed between themselves trying to guess the reason for the meeting, common consensus being that the Oubaas was leaving the farm and the important black man sitting next to him was the new owner. But then again, they were not sure how a black man could obtain or own land outside a communal area or homeland.

After an hour, his father asked for quiet.

'I am ready to give you the important news.'

Mr Matanzima was then introduced to the group as a clever man who had studied overseas and who had helped him in what he was about to say.

'Much planning had been done, many nights I have not slept well. Many times I wonder if what I am telling you is the right thing to do.'

He hoped the group would understand what he had to say and that they would support him, and each other, in accepting the proposal that he was going to make.

He told them of his family's roots. How his great ancestors had come to Africa in small boats, so many years ago. How they had suffered, had been sick; and then settled on this farm without the prospect of ever returning to where they came from.

In an African story-telling manner, sometimes glossing over the important, sometimes detailing the unimportant, he led them through the development of the farm. Which generation had built the house, which generation laid out the water piping and erected the original fences, who had divined water holes and wells; where the first cattle had come from and in which year the first calves had been born.

They were reminded of the wild animals being reintroduced, with the large eland, the gentle kudu, the lively impala - all now free and doing well and having calves, bringing natural beauty for everyone to look at.

He spoke of his worries for the future, about the Soweto riots in Johannesburg, that the white government was ostracized, the sports teams were isolated. Violence between black man and white man; black against black man was on the increase, and that tribalism was a big problem, Zulu against Xhosa and Sotho against Tswana.

'I do not know if and when Mr Mandela will be released, the longer this takes the more it concerns me.'

Mr Mandela was one of their own, a Xhosa man; he was important to the future.

Then he stopped talking. The gathering of people was spellbound, his wife silently weeping, she in the knowledge of what he was about to say, knowing what he was about to give up.

Slowly the children were hushed. An elderly farm labourer stood up and instructed one of the young girls, 'Nonyameko, keep the little ones together and quiet.'

He thanked the Oubaas and said, 'we, the people, see you as our father; we are ready to hear your proposal, which you said would be important to all our futures.'

And then, with the firelight reflecting off the black faces and his wife's tears glistening on her cheeks, the white farmer told his people, his black employees, that he was going to give them half of all he owned.

'The land, the buildings, the tractors and trucks, cattle and game, all shall be shared. Lily the housemaid, Festus the gardener, the old labourer Jackson who is your spokesperson, the cattle herders, the tractor driver and the people who look after the tourists; all will join me in owning the farm.'

It may be difficult to understand. There would be conditions to the ownership. Mr Matanzima would explain it and anybody could ask questions.

There was a short moment of silence and then clamour.

Everyone wanted to speak. Whether to each other or across to the white farmer, there were shouted, animated questions and comments. The magnitude of the offer seemed only to be understood by Jackson. Even though he was totally unschooled and illiterate, he remained calm. For a while he allowed the excitement to continue, then, when there was a lull, he stood up slowly.

The old labourer raised his hand and the assembly quietened down. He looked at the farmer. Dryly he said, 'Oubaas must be quite mad, to be doing a thing like this. No black man would ever give half of his possessions away. Even when they give their daughters away in marriage, lobola has to be paid back to the father. The new son-in-law has to pay with cattle and goods, even money. It is not normal to us to receive such a large gift, a farm! For nothing.'

But Jackson thought that he understood and would help Mr Matanzima talk to the people.

'It is not for nothing. It is for peace and harmony. For us all,' the white man asserted quietly, when he thanked them all again.

★★★

After the second meeting a week later, every employee had signed, or in some cases thumb printed the contractual document. There had not been a single dissenting person. The conditions had been gone over and over again. An individual's shareholding could not be sold without all shareholders reaching agreement as to the value and to whom it was being sold. Improvements and alterations to the farm could only be done with seventy percent of the shareholders agreeing;

similarly to the purchasing of new equipment, increasing and decreasing herd sizes. Shareholders always had to live on, work on and protect the farm. The distribution of profit, the understanding and dealing with loss, monthly accounts, annual balance sheet, general meetings and special meetings - all were included in the contract.

The share being retained by the white family would entitle them to manage the farm and live in the main farmhouse, all in perpetuity.

Leigh Ann listened through it all. At the end she stated, 'that is amazing. What about the conservatives, the verkramptes, the other farmers?'

'When word circulated in the district, my father was inundated with visits and telephone calls from his neighbours, to a person appalled by what he had done. Articles appeared in the local white owned newspapers, letters were written to editors, anonymous threats of vengeance uttered.'

'That he had gone ahead without consulting them was a major issue. But my old man reminded them all - black people are hungry for land, white farmers want to remain on the land, something has to be done. I believe that I've done the right thing.'

Cathan continued. 'Time will prove this, and in years to come the farm should continue to thrive; hopefully never to be targeted for violence or squatting. There is always a harmonious, no that's the wrong word, a settled aura surrounding it.'

Leigh spoke of her lifestyle in Johannesburg, the theatres, dining out, garden parties and tennis clubs. Her marriage to Jack, fifteen years her senior, was childless, a decision they had consciously made, although she could not really remember why. Jack was a neurosurgeon and had inherited wealth, liked to travel and especially to follow sports tours around. But her own life was more in the socialite set and had become too organised, too sedentary.

They cleared the table and moved into the lounge. Whilst he selected Mozart's beautiful K 478, she settled herself on the large couch facing the window and the sound of the sea. He sat across from her, looking at her with those great eyes and she knew that she was drowning into him.

The telephone on the side table next to Leigh Ann rang. It was his mother calling in from the farm. Cathan turned the music down and chatted to her. They spoke of the weather and the state of the bushveld; the condition of the livestock and game animals.

'Why don't you come and visit me?' his mother asked, 'your Dad is going away next week, to an agricultural show. Just stay over for a night, it would be great to see you!'

As Cathan stood there talking, his right hand moved down onto Leigh Ann's shoulder and then to her neck, just touching subtly, including her in the conversation.

And she moved her head to rest on his thigh; she was falling in love for the first time in her life and would be lost to him for the remainder of her life.

He ended off to his mother with a promise to visit her the next week and would she mind if he possibly brought a guest along, a neighbour of his on Millionaires' Mile?

'No problem, look forward to seeing you next week,' she said gaily and rang off.

Both his hands were on her shoulders now; he could feel her shivering under his touch.

'Oh Cathan, what is happening to me,' she whispered, 'what is happening?'

He bent down and kissed the nape of her neck, and then moved around to sit beside her on the couch. Mozart's piano quartet wafted peacefully across the room. He took her in his arms, encircled them around her, held her strongly, her head on his chest.

She lifted her face and then they kissed, a long searching and lingering kiss, exploring each other's lips and mouths, down each other's necks. He held her and she moved her hands on him, feeling his shoulders and arms, the sides of his waist and down to the strength of his thighs. They kissed again; with her arms wrapped around him she allowed his hands to feel her, fondling her shoulders, the insides of her arms through the blouse, down her legs and then back up again.

Moving slightly apart, they caught their breaths. He smiled at her and she at him.

'Cathan, would you mind if I lie on the couch a little while you hold me some more?' she asked.

They were like this when she drifted off to sleep; the ocean air and the day, the emotions and feelings, all catching up with her.

As dawn was breaking she awoke, finding herself still on the couch and covered with a blanket. She looked down and saw that Cathan was asleep on the floor beside her. Their hands were entwined, her right hand hanging over the edge of the couch holding his left hand, which was resting on his chest. Leigh Ann lay there looking at him, he relaxed and almost not breathing, so lightly was he sleeping. Then he opened his eyes and smiled at her, and she thought that her heart would burst.

He drifted off again. When he awoke she was gone. There were faint noises in the kitchen, and the smell of fresh coffee came drifting through. Cathan padded through and squatted on his haunches in the kitchen's doorway, watching her. She was unaware of him as she washed the few dishes from their dinner, tidying up the kitchen, softly singing John Lennon's 'Imagine' in a surprisingly melodious voice. In a world of her own, she pottered on. Cathan watched and admired what he saw; her blouse hanging free and her hair tousled. Below her waist, her jeans encasing large shapely buttocks, well defined legs and calves. The coffee brewed, she turned to pour herself a cup and that was when she saw him, silently observing her.

She giggled as he put his arms around her and they kissed again. An early morning kiss that left them breathless and laughing.

They took their coffee to the patio, she told him that she could not remember when she had last slept so well.

'How could you have been comfortable on the floor?'

'I'm used to it, often sleep on the ground when out camping in the veld, or when sleeping at home on the hot nights.'

As the sun rose over the sea, and holding hands lightly, they planned their first full day together.

They went running together on the beach with their dogs bounding out in front of them. He jogged with her at her pace. Again she watched him, admiring his athletic body, the ease of his stride and its natural fluidity.

It was his day to work in the garden. After a light breakfast, she went off to do some shopping and he joined the old man. They were in good spirits and the morning flew past. When Leigh Ann returned Joshua looked up, greeted her, and she smiled at him in response.

Curiosity was consuming the old man. As he was finishing up for the day, he muttered: 'so young Cathan has a very beautiful auntie?'

And Cathan replied, laughing, 'she is beautiful, but definitely not my aunt.'

And Old Joshua grinned, a gap toothed know-it-all grin. 'I already know who she is, I've worked in this area for the last fifteen years. The beautiful lady lives just down the road.'

The afternoon was spent on the beach, Leigh Ann insistent on wanting to surf again. He helped her and watched her; she was more daring now, trying out the larger waves. Sometimes she fell off quite spectacularly, but always came up laughing, or more often than not, more spluttering than laughing.

He looked at her more openly now. In her black bikini, drying off in the warm sunlight, her body was rounded and lush. Her breasts bulged over the bikini top and her derriere full; he wanted to touch her, but knew that it was wise to wait, not to rush, and upset what was happening to them.

That evening they went to bed together but still did not make love. They lay entwined, she in an old tee-shirt of his, kissing and caressing for a long time. In the dark his hands roamed her body, always gentle and her hands roamed his, feeling his muscularity and strength.

His self control and maturity continued to amaze her; she could feel that he was fully erect and highly aroused, but all he murmured was, 'let's take our time and be patient; and when we are completely ready.'

He was right of course; she was in emotional turmoil; in love, excited and aroused and yet feeling guilty all at the same time. She was married to someone else and forty- six years old, he was a young man of twenty-one.

Wrapped around each other they fell asleep and Leigh Ann was comfortable. During the night she awoke and when she turned to face him, he was looking at her fondly. Cathan kissed her softly; she fell asleep again, her uncertainty gone and her mind at ease.

It was the noise of water that awoke her; Cathan was in the shower and now it was her chance to watch him. But he knew she was there. When he emerged from the shower he grinned, 'Peeping Tom', and she had the temerity to blush before hugging him.

'Go to bed and wait for me,' she whispered.

She showered quickly and then was with him.

He studied her body; her large breasts sagging slightly but wonderful to look at, with large aureolae and nipples. Her pubic patch was full and thick, as dark as the hair on her head; her skin was silk smooth, unblemished and beautiful.

'You are so lovely,' he said softly, 'I will never last.'

'Shh, my darling, let's do this my way.'

And she took his engorged penis in her hand and gently masturbated him.

Within minutes, he came with a groan of pleasure.

And then Leigh Ann showed him what she liked and as she began to breathe heavily, he was hard again. Pulling him on top of her, they joined and made love together. She came shuddering to orgasm, calling out his name 'Oh Cathan, oh my darling. Oh Cathan!'

And he again just after.

They lay languorous for a long time, murmuring those little endearments that lovers do, kissing and holding each other. She told him that she loved him, he looked into her eyes and into her being, and knew it to be true.

★★★

They jogged on the beach and exercised their dogs. Cathan taught her how to run properly, keeping her head still, getting her arms to move evenly at her sides, breathing smoothly in and out, to coincide with her steps. She was soon able to increase her distances and vary her pace, sometimes doing longer slower distances and at other times alternating - running quickly for short distances and resting by jogging slowly in between.

In the afternoons they would be in the sea; he taught her how to paddle-ski. While he surfed, Leigh Ann would paddle in deeper water just beyond the waves, close to him. She was scared the first time the dolphins appeared around them. Cathan paddled his surfboard over to her, held it up against her ski.

'Just be calm,' he said.

And as they lay on the surface of the water, she realised that the dolphins appeared to seek the humans out, in a friendly social manner. There were about twelve in all. To her amazement one of them swam close to Cathan and he was able to touch it - the dolphin almost motionless next to him. Out there on the calm sea she heard the animal chirping softly. And then it calmly swam away.

Cathan spoke, 'listen carefully.'

She realised that she could hear clicks and whistling sounds as the marine animals talked to each other.

'I have read reports of dolphins coming to help swimmers who get into distress. The dolphins push them closer to shore, or even try to protect them from shark attacks,' he told her.

'There are cases of people suffering from certain mental illnesses who become better after swimming with dolphins in the wild.'

'How can that be explained?' Leigh Ann queried.

'I don't know, nobody really knows. Maybe they improve because the tactile pleasure of an such experience is so uplifting. Perhaps the ultra-sonic sounds that dolphins make may have a healing effect.'

'It's just wonderful,' she said.

***

They arose early one morning and drove north to the forests, from there onwards to the family farm. Cathan had arranged for the two servants to come in for the time that he was away. In view of his concessions for all their time off, he was re-assured that they would look after the house and dog in his absence. A local security company was contacted to also visit the premises from time to time. He felt at ease on leaving that morning.

By late morning they were already walking on a trail in the forests, following a guide pamphlet that they had collected from the forest station. It was surprising to Leigh Ann that the undergrowth, and the forest itself, was not that dense. The trees, many of them huge, were well spaced, with open areas in between.

And of course, there was Cathan with his knowledge and interest. He pointed out the great South African trees, the yellow-woods, stinkwoods and blackwoods, the camphors and olives, the tambuti. Some of them the loggers were allowed to cut down after a certain age for joinery and furniture making, others had to have fallen before they could be logged.

She watched him as he moved through the forest. He was almost silent, did not disturb the growth; aware of all going on around them. At the edge of a small clearing he showed her a bushbuck feeding on some leaves; it was an attractive male, dark brown in colour, with white spots on its legs and white patches on the throat and at the base of its neck. The horns were surprisingly large and solid, slightly twirled and symmetrically uniform and lovely.

Further on he stopped.

'Look carefully, it's very difficult to see,' he whispered.

'What is it?'

'A blue duiker.'

'It's so small.'

'Yes, but fully grown.'

There was a gleam of sunlight shining through the

leaves down onto the dainty little antelope and they could see the blue-ish sheen on its back.

Above them, there was a slow 'kerk-kerk-kerk-kawk-kawk-kawk' call, and they watched a pair of knysna louries, jumping along the branches of a large yellowwood tree. The birds were wonderfully coloured, green torsos, azure blue tails and pretty heads with white markings around the eyes. But when they flew their true beauty was revealed, brilliant full crimson coloured wings.

They spent the night at a small village inn, with the middle-aged landlady giving them a country dinner of river trout and locally grown vegetables. Her eyes had widened slightly when she served them, saw them holding hands across the dinner table. But she was gracious and helpful, and seemed a little envious.

'I am looking forward to meeting your mother. Also apprehensive as well,' Leigh Ann said.

'No, don't worry, she's very tolerant, will understand.'

'What is she like?'

'Well...she's a little different. Not your normal farmer's wife.' Cathan sat back in his chair. 'Although Mom was born on the adjacent farm and married Dad when she was eighteen, she still studied on by correspondence. Did her first degree by the time my sister was born, finished her honours before I was born. She's widely read - can speak fluent English, Afrikaans, German and Xhosa and her intelligence is unbounded. She is constantly learning new things: pottery, painting, even carpentry.'

Leigh Ann studied his face. 'You admire her very much.'

'Oh, I do, and love her very much too.' He paused, 'you know she's also very politically aware. Mom carefully follows the political events of the apartheid government and years before they were to occur, would tell us of changes that would come.'

'The western governments will force the Nationalist Party to its knees, she would say. Embargoes and economic sanctions will be stronger than so-called freedom fighters trying to defeat the South African Army.'

'Mom tells us that the black peoples want true freedom and the devolution of white supremacy. There will be corruption, increased poverty, violence, crime, the illnesses and diseases.'

'She thinks that a public reconciliation process will take place, which may assuage some of the hurt between the race groups. An emotional blood letting that might give South Africa a fresh start; she has an understanding and time frame for it all. As time may later prove, I am sure she will be exactly right.'

Cathan continued. 'Where my father institutes order to the farm, my mother generates the planning and future thought for her loved ones. Her encouragement led to us three children developing differently. Along the paths of our talents, not shackled by prospects of traditional farming life.'

★★★

They reached the farm just after noon the following day. Cathan's mother was the next person with widened eyes, but at the same time also equally welcoming and friendly.

He left the two women to get to know each other and toured the farm in an open Landrover, one that his father used to ferry the tourists around in.

Everything was spic and span, the gates neatly painted, fences taut, mechanical installations in good order and serviced. For early summer, the veld was in fair condition and he saw that his father's land management practices were as sound as ever. The grass was short but not overgrazed, the bush had been held in check through derooting and judicious burning. He greeted the odd worker that he saw and left messages for those who wanted to, to visit him at the farmhouse in early evening.

As he made the external fire, Cathan could hear his mother and Leigh Ann chattering and giggling like schoolgirls. He grinned to himself. Earlier he had mischievously suggested to Leigh Ann that they could go horse-riding the next morning.

'We have a placid old mare for a placid old...,' not quite finishing the impudence.

No doubt, this had been repeated to his mother as well.

After they had barbecued their meat and eaten their dinner, the three sat at the fireside under the trees. The workers came down as invited. In ones and twos they sat with Cathan and told him of the recent happenings on the farm and in the area. The two white women sat quietly as the others talked. Leigh Ann was impressed with the contentment and respect that the black people showed, but then she saw that it was a mutual thing. Cathan was thoughtful in his questions and discussions, never critical of an individual. His respect for the people was as great as theirs for him.

Leigh Ann mused on how so young a person could know and achieve this; her love was now so great and so deep and she longed to talk to his mother about him. But this was not the time or the place.

They slept in separate bedrooms that night.

At dawn Cathan and Leigh Ann rode out on horseback, following a trail that led from the farmhouse for some two miles to the top of a small hill, the highest point on the farm. Sitting on their horses and watching the rays of the early morning sun breaking across the veld, the colours soft oranges and yellows, they heard the quiet calls of the birds; cattle noise in the distance. On top of the hill Cathan turned to look at her and there for the first time, he told her that he loved her, deeply and truly, his great eyes looking on her, into her and through her.

She examined him with her own brilliant blue eyes, smiled, and then was crying.

With tears streaming she said, 'I am so happy, never been happier. I've never loved like this..., learnt like this..., lived like this..., felt like this.'

Even the horses could sense the emotion of the moment and sidled together, nuzzling, gently bumping each other. Cathan leant across them and held Leigh Ann in his arms. The moment was pure and for all time.

For a while they sat; in that still, clear morning, accompanied only by the gentle blowing sounds of the horses and occasional bird sounds.

When Leigh Ann had composed herself, the two of

them moved down to the farmstead to have breakfast with Cathan's mother. Being as perceptive as ever, Cathan's mother quickly sensed the emotional mood. She eased the conversation around the goings on in the district, relating light-hearted incidents involving neighbours. The dyslexic son of their nearest neighbour, a lad of twelve, had recently created havoc at a ladies' tea party, held at his parents farmhouse.

'You know Bertus, Jan van Niekerk's son?' she asked Cathan.

'Well, just before the party he removed all the screws and dowels from the small tables and then carefully re-balanced the tops on the legs. As you can imagine, when tea was served there was chaos.'

By the time they were ready to leave, everyone was smiling and cheerful.

In the short time they had spent together, the two women had quickly developed a genuine liking and affinity for each other. With their adoration for Cathan, one as a mother, one as a lover, being the cord that drew them together.

But when his mother hugged him goodbye, all she very quietly said was, 'her heart will break.'

★★★

Any last reserve previously between them was now gone. His avowal of love to her had seen to that. Their days were spent exploring each other's minds and bodies, and the immediate world around them.

When the weather was cool or rainy, they would visit

the surrounding villages. Small museums were of interest to him; especially the displays and records pertaining to the migration of black peoples into east and southern Africa. The manner in which the local Hottentots and San peoples were subjugated and persecuted by the invading migrants, and then later in turn, the colonisation of the Cape of Good Hope by the Dutch, the French and the English, which resulted in further conflict with the black peoples. As the emerging Afrikaners moved north, away from foreign rule to seek a freedom of their own, subjugation and persecution turned another cog.

'I hope you don't find this all too boring,' Cathan would say, on more than one occasion. But she didn't, the old chronicles were fascinating. Great hunting parties decimated the wildlife; the San and Koisan peoples were viewed as fair game, the trekking Afrikaners knew no bounds.

Cathan would pore over the information, pictures and photographs, making copious notes, all in an endeavour to comprehend what had happened. By the year 1842, in a mere ten years, all the grazing and browsing antelopes were wiped out. The great predators were exterminated, the lion, cheetah and leopards - all the hippopotamus; a few elephants survived, retreating deep into the forests. Thousands upon thousands of animals were killed, certain species taken to extinction. Left teetering on the brink were the white and black rhinoceros, a few bontebuck, mountain zebra and black wildebeest.

Even more startling was what happened to the San or Bushman peoples. The few that managed to escape fled deep into the dry hinterland - some to the most remote areas of Bechuanaland and South West Africa, the present day countries known as Botswana and Namibia.

All this had a profound effect on Cathan. In the evenings as he and Leigh Ann talked, they would debate the motives of settlers.

'Why did they do this? Denude the land of life, destroy resources that were of no threat. And not only here. Australia, New Zealand, the Americas, wherever Europeans went. And they were supposed to be educated, intelligent people. No wonder the resentment is so deep.'

And Cathan reminded Leigh Ann of his intentions for the future, to try and live and work in remote areas among peoples who were still in close contact with nature and the land. Slightly wistful, she would look at him.

'My darling, there must be places to go to, discover them, live with the nomads, live marginalized, learn to understand their situations and then help them to cope. Do research, go to the authorities, make public your findings. Get the aid organisations to assist you. Make your intelligence and knowledge mean something.'

And then she would draw close to him, to hide what she felt inside, realising that he would do it, aware he would be living a life that she had no part in.

★★★

There were just under three weeks to go before Cathan's housekeeping duties were up and he was due to return to college. He awoke some mornings to find Leigh Ann out walking alone on the beach. No intrusion was necessary; he knew that she was thinking of their pending separation, which they knew in their hearts would probably be final and forever.

They had spoken of it and whilst she had said that she would cope, he sensed that the eventual outcome would be traumatic. Even when talking openly about it, her tear-filled eyes and tremulous voice betrayed her.

A depression would sink into her. When this happened he would hold her close, soothing her with quiet words of care. He said that they were no longer the same two individuals they had been before they had met. A new entity had come into place, that of he and she together, a oneness, that could be physically separated, but who remain together in spirit and being forever.

'But Cathan you are young, I will never see you again, you may find someone else and then what of me.'

Into her ears, his reply was always the same.

'It doesn't matter where we are, you and I are now one person, a new being. We have been together and done things together, our bodies and minds have merged, nothing can change this. If it so happens that you, or I, find someone else in whatever circumstances or for whatever reason, if love with that person is pure and true, another new oneness will be created. Not displacing us or taking away what we have become.'

And the night would be spent talking and making love. They would tell each other of childhood experiences and of going to school, relating stories of families and friends, of their pets and early interests. She felt that the superficiality and wealth of her married life had suppressed her dreams and ambitions. Being married to a much older man, not having children, had left her unfulfilled in some way. In the depths of the night, when he lay over her and in her, she would talk and talk. It was as if she was clearing out her life before him, setting herself free for the times ahead when she knew that she would be alone.

***

They had a fortnight left together. She sprang a surprise on him on the penultimate Friday. The house servants had arrived to look after the property at her request, looking somewhat smug as she had obviously told them of her plan.

Cathan was persuaded to pack a bag and then Leigh Ann drove them to the local aerodrome to catch a flight to Cape Town.

'I want to show you how the South African wealthy live and what I have experienced, so different to what you know; my treat, no expenses spared.'

She laughed at his apprehensive face and hugged him, 'you have given me so much, so many new things, new experiences, let me also do a little in return. It may be ostentatious and it will probably be my materialistic swanswong, but let's just enjoy what I have arranged.'

She had booked them into the Mount Nelson in Cape Town, an opulent, colonial hotel set in glorious gardens, close to the centre of the city. Their suite was luxurious in the extreme, all the furnishings in the best of taste. A jacuzzi with a glass roof was situated adjacent to the bathroom. The large bedroom featured a huge antique four poster bed.

On their arrival, they were met by an ebullient Xhosa doorman and an equally happy porter.

'Good Day, Sir and Madam, welcome to the best hotel in Africa,' the doorman had boomed. 'And how lovely your mother looks,' he said to Cathan.

But with a little grin, Cathan replied in the Xhosa language, that the lady was indeed very lovely, was more like a number one wife; definitely not his mother.

For a moment the wind was taken completely out of the black man's sails and then he was even more welcoming. The three men were all smiling now, shaking hands and extending greetings in the African style, while Leigh Ann stood and watched, not understanding a word that was being said.

From then on and for the rest of their stay, the black staff at the hotel treated them like royalty. Leigh Ann could not quite comprehend this.

'The staff are always very courteous and efficient, but this is exceptional; what did you say to those two?' she asked Cathan at the end of their stay.

'My lips are sealed,' was his reply to her.

★★★

Cathan was concerned for her that she might meet people that she knew. But she shrugged it aside.

'I will deal with any situation that arises. And anyway my life has changed forever.'

In the event it was a wonderful weekend with no awkward occurrences.

He took pleasure in her happiness, her secret

assignations, which she would not tell him of in advance. All Leigh Ann did was tell him what to wear.

She took him to an elegant seafood restaurant on the first evening, where they shared a fine crayfish platter and smooth chardonnay wine. Not talking much, just holding hands and looking at each other. She indelibly imprinting his face and features on her brain, he marvelling in her beauty and love for him.

Early the next morning, she called for a taxi. After a quiet word with the driver, they were driven through the vineyards of the scenic Franschoek Valley, following the winding road up the mountainside to a level clearing. There, to Cathan's amusement, a hot air balloon was rigged up, with a pilot-cum-guide waiting for them.

The taxi was despatched back to city. In minutes they were ascending.

'Another little surprise, my sweet,' Leigh Ann giggled; then they were both laughing and kissing, much to the amusement of the pilot who clearly had not realised that the two were lovers.

They floated out over the mountain crest, across the summit and towards Cape Point, the meeting place of the Indian and Atlantic Oceans.

The views were stunning. Looking back towards the mountains, the crags and peaks were purple and golden in the early light.

Suddenly gliding next to them were a pair of Verreaux's eagles, glorious large black eagles endemic to the Southern African mountainous areas. Through the pilot's binoculars Cathan watched them swirl and circle. At the same time he narrated his knowledge of these wonderful birds, how they mated for life, usually producing two chicks at a time of which only one would be fortunate to survive. Their nests were huge constructions of jumbled sticks, perched high up on the mountains ledges and crevices.

He told of their hunting habits, their prey being the rock hyrax or dassie which comprised ninety percent of their diet. These little rock rabbits were equally interesting. Strangely their nearest animal relatives were elephants, to which they were linked by the similarity of their spinal structures. He explained how the rabbits could scurry around the rock faces, because their feet were kept moist by glandular secretions in the soles which helped them to grip.

But getting back to the eagles' hunting techniques he said, 'the leading eagle will spot a dassie sunning itself on a ledge, swoop down on it and feign attack; the dassie will retreat to safety under the ledge. Then, when it thinks that the danger is over, it will emerge. With perfect timing the second bird will grab the dassie off the ledge, all in a matter of seconds.'

They were over the ocean now; the sea fairly calm, with a blue tranquillity masking the currents, deceiving the eye.

Looking down, the pilot pointed to a large fish shoal to the left. 'Look behind the shoal, look carefully through the binoculars. Tell me what you can see?' he asked.

Cathan with his sharp eyesight and affinity to nature quickly detected the larger shapes lurking on the fringes of the shoal. As he pointed them out to Leigh Ann, the pilot told them that they were probably fish eating sharks, ragged tooth known as raggies and tiger sharks, maybe even a few blues which he had seen occasionally.

'What about the great whites?' she asked.

'Not at this time of the year,' the pilot replied, adding, 'the great whites feed mainly on seal pups, rather than fish. Normally during the middle of the year they can be seen hunting around the seal islands off the Cape coast.'

The pilot guided the balloon across False Bay, the naval base of Simonstown passing on their right hand side. The sea cliffs of Cape Point were ahead of them. These sea cliffs, of the highest in the world, are an awesome formation for the merging of two oceans. Before the Point was reached, they started to cross the peninsula and headed north past Table Mountain with its vistas and views: Signal Hill, Lions Head and Twelve Apostles.

'The Fairest Cape of All,' the pilot said and it was, on a morning like that, early in a summer's day. The beautiful Table Bay was beneath them and Robben Island in the northwest, ahead of them to their left. Robben Island, prison to Nelson Mandela for so many years.

They drifted on slowly downwards, landing in a field where the pilot's wife was waiting for them. The balloon was deflated and loaded onto a specially designed trailer. Leigh Ann and Cathan were returned to their hotel.

The exhilaration of the flight and the beauty of the day had overwhelmed them. Leigh Ann's face was glowing and she was like a young exuberant girl, whilst Cathan had a serene calmness about him. They stood on their balcony overlooking the magnificent gardens, their arms around each other, Leigh Ann whispering, 'I Love You, I love you, oh I love you my darling,' over and over and over.

The afternoon was spent alongside the pool. Leigh Ann was spectacular in her black swimsuit. Two months of exercise and being in the outdoors had firmed her body, toned the muscles of her stomach, legs and arms. Cathan watched with quiet pride the looks she received from the various men and women who were sunning themselves.

Some of the men were open in their admiration, whilst others surreptitiously looked from under their hats or behind their newspapers. When she walked around the pool, her breasts quivering lightly under the top, buttocks firmly muscled and rounded in the bikini bottom, she was a picture of health and sensuality.

After dinner that evening she led Cathan on to another of her surprises. Earlier she had made him dress fairly formally in jacket and tie; she donned an elegant black dress, open down her back, simple gold bracelet and matching shawl; high-heeled black shoes completed the outfit.

The surprise was the local Symphony Orchestra performing Beethoven at the Malan Theatre. She was radiant when she accompanied him into the venue. They were a strikingly attractive couple, amidst a throng of happy people. It was the music that enthralled Cathan. Completely engrossed in the melodious complexity, Beethoven's Emperor Concerto washed over and through him. And when Leigh Ann looked at him, observing his enjoyment and pleasure, her happiness in that moment was absolute.

They went to bed that night in a state of repleted bliss. He held her in his arms and they slept in complete peace.

***

Their last few days together were spent in a state of emotive anxiety. The realisation that they would separate, probably forever, led them to be happy and then sad all at the same time. Cathan with his natural composure and presence, and with the immediate future mapped out before him, was better able to cope. But Leigh Ann steadily became more and more distraught. She would be singing and buoyant, but after a moment's reflection, her eyes would brim with tears. He held and comforted her, but it was as if her life spirit was steadily being blown out.

'I knew this time would come, I thought that I could deal with it,' she wept to him, 'what little I know of myself.'

They went on long walks together, to try and deal with their sadness; miles strolling along the beaches, over the littoral dunes, through the woodland areas. Miles of holding hands, or arms around each other's waists, not talking much, just absorbed in their love. Occasionally Cathan would point out a bird, or a dolphin in the waves, a delicate coastal flower, and she would look at him and sadly smile.

'I will always adore you, will always remember you, will die loving you,' she whispered.

Moving a mattress out onto the patio, they spent their last night together. Not sleeping, just talking, holding each other, she sometimes sobbing quietly. For a last time they made gentle tender love; under the stars, with a soft sea breeze blowing over them.

And as he lay with Leigh Ann, consoling her, Cathan reminded her of their oneness, this entity they had become and of how he loved her.

'If you ever need me in the future, if you are desperate, in distress, I will come to you.'

Over and over he repeated that he would always be there for her. She should use the knowledge of his love to sustain her, she should face the future in hope, remembering the time that they had been together, to have met and shared and loved. To have learnt of each other and from each other.

In the early morning they parted. Holding each other for a long time; he kissed her for a last time, looked intently at her, placed a small locket around her neck. Leigh Ann was crying openly now, all resolve to remain controlled had disappeared; tears were running down his cheeks as well.

'I love you, my dearest', he said.

He waved once as he drove around the corner and then was lost from view. Was gone.

She sank to the sidewalk after his departure, all strength depleted. Opening the locket Cathan had given her, she saw that a goldsmith had skilfully intertwined their names in a delicate filigree. Unable to contain herself anymore, Leigh Ann sat there, head between knees, weeping.

Eventually old Joshua came to her aid; lifted her up. Half supporting and trying to calm her at the same time, he assisted her home.

★★★

August 1991

The two men had been tracking the group for four days.

The matriarch led the six elephants down the Hoanib River towards the sea. Some fifteen miles short of the coast she turned northward, following her own well-worn tracks and those of her predecessors. Maintaining a steady pace, the group had covered a hundred kilometres during the time that Cathan and Bird had been following them. From waterhole to waterhole the elephants walked, doing the majority of the distance at night; slowing down during the hot days, foraging for food and resting in the shade of the large camelthorn trees.

At the start of this, his first field trip, Cathan had been determined to observe the elephants in a very scientific, neutral way. The group was to be numbered in his notes, each individual being identified as 'Group 1/Male or Female/Adult, Infant/ characteristic.' The larger male in this group would be G1/M/A/ Notched Ear. Only factual notes would be recorded of the elephant's behaviour, traits and physical characteristics.

Cathan explained this process to Bird who looked at him rather quizzically.

'I think you will soon change your mind. Then your notes will become far more interesting ….and personal,' the coloured man stated.

Early on the fourth day, the group descended into the Hoarusib river valley and made their way to a pool of water. The younger animals went to drink straight away, but the old matriarch stood aside, looking back along the track that they had walked. It was as if she were waiting for Cathan to come into view. She was not afraid or concerned; her senses told her that there was no threat. Her intelligence perceived that they were being observed for their own good. The men's aura was tolerant and protective.

Could she sense that a bond was developing between them, some invisible thread of mutual trust and respect? Cathan voiced this to Bird, who very seriously agreed.

'Elephants are generally wiser than most of the people I know, with the possible exception of my young white colleague here.' His straight face wrinkled into a small grin.

When Cathan and Bird drove slowly into view and stopped, the big elephant turned and went to drink. As predicted, Cathan's field notes were already more personal. The matriarch they named Meme, an Ovambo name meaning 'respected mother'. Older than fifty years, she was clearly the leader and guardian, probably just beyond calf bearing age. There were three younger females, each about fifteen to twenty years old, two with little calves of their own which they were nursing.

The remaining elephant was an adult male of medium age. It seemed as if he was slightly retarded and almost blind. Watching him, the men saw that the larger of the females, the one without a calf, was always close to him. She nudged him along at times, guiding him carefully through the rougher terrain when needed, leading him to the leafier trees to browse. Carefully gentle with the little ones when they came near him, he was big and clumsy and simple.

It was Bird who noticed it; a scar on the left side of his great head, close to the eye.

'Probably a bullet wound, from a poachers or soldier's rifle – it's possible that the bullet is still lodged in his head, this has affected him,' was his view.

From then on the large animal's epithet became a slightly ironical but not disrespectful Bullit.

★★★

In an area exceeding 38,000 square kilometres or 24,000 square miles, they were the only two official conservation officers. A privately funded wildlife society had a third person working in the area; the fourth, a German anthropologist, was studying the local Himba peoples.

The Kaokoveld. A land of mountains and plains, of extreme daytime heat and severe winter night cold. Once populous with game and cattle, the region now denuded by protracted drought, poachers and the South African Defence Force.

A vast area, a last wilderness, bordered in the north by the Kunene river and Angola; the Skeleton Coast and Atlantic Ocean to the west, the Etosha Game Reserve and Ovambo region to the east; the south another forbidding area called Damaraland.

It was an expanse sustained by the permanently flowing Kunene River on the northern border, and other occasional annual rivers. The Khumib, Hoarusib, Hoanib, Uniab, Koigab, Huab and the southernmost Ugab were the lifeblood; flooding after heavy rains, otherwise dry with a few waterholes and springs. Known only to the Himba people and the remaining wildlife, additional waterholes and ponds could be found in the remotest mountain valleys.

The Kaokoveld is distant and desolate, pristine and beautiful.

***

May 1991

His superior, a loud hardbitten chief conservation officer at headquarters in Windhoek had recommended that they set up a permanent camp at one of the more central, now vacated South African Defence Force bases. Nevertheless, he was of no fixed view. His requirements were easy to satisfy.

'I need a monthly written report and a quarterly field trip survey. Don't make them too long, nobody ever reads the bloody things. But I do want to speak to you, every fortnight. By radio via the telecoms centre in Walvis Bay!'

Their bulk supplies and provisions could be purchased on account from the government store in Opuwo, the only town of substance in the area.

'And don't go over your budget! Then I get into the shit, with you sliding in after me!'

From the main store in Windhoek, Cathan requisitioned all the practical equipment he could think of, tools and vehicle spares, radios and antennae, a comprehensive first- aid kit, and an array of odds and ends that he thought would be needed.

The coloured man allocated to accompany him as his assistant was a short, wizened fellow who, as Cathan later found out, was of mixed parentage, Herero father and San mother. The little man's linguistic ability was phenomenal. Fluent in at least five local languages, he could also speak English fairly well, Afrikaans and a smattering of German. His introduction to Cathan was simple and straightforward.

'I will be your eyes and ears; you will be my captain, *my kaptein*. My name is Bird. My people call me by this name because they say I have the sight and hearing of an eagle. It is probably a very small black eagle.'

Both men laughed at this and the following day they were on their way.

It was three days later when they arrived at Swartbooisdrift, Cathan in a Landrover pickup pulling a trailer, Bird driving an old but well maintained 7-ton truck - both vehicles loaded to capacity. In Windhoek the two men had studied maps of the Kaokoveld for hours, choosing where to establish their base camp.

In the end, it was Bird who decided it. 'We need a permanent water supply and firewood, nothing less. The boss might want us to be centrally situated, but to what end? The roads are bad, mainly rocky or deep sand tracks, the distances are so great; we may as well have some available resources to help us. If something goes very wrong, we also need to be within a day's journey of a village where we might get help.'

They expected to find a few inhabitants in the region, some local people having re-established there again after the remaining South African troops had withdrawn the previous year. Or perhaps a nomadic Himba group with its cattle and goats or a geologist's camp. But the entire area was deserted. Even though they had the required authority to establish their camp at Swartbooisdrift, the two men had fully expected to consult with any local people before settling in.

There was no one to talk to, no protocol to follow.

An abandoned building stood in a clearing some fifty metres from the river's edge. It had no doors or windows, merely openings, but the walls were thick and solid and the roof still intact, sheeted with old, rusty corrugated iron. This became their base camp.

***

June 1993

The sun had just set. Along the western horizon the yellow glow was changing to orange and then slowly to umber.

It was early winter in the Kaokoveld. But the desert does not show the change in seasons as obviously as in other climes. Trees in the water courses remain green; if there is grass on the plains it is yellow as generally throughout the year. Only when rains come does everything change, desert flowers bloom and the new grass is a glorious green.

Seasonal difference is evidenced in the temperature. The days are still hot, as much as 35°C, but the nights turn icy. In summer the temperature at night is very warm, maybe 10°C off the day's high of 40°C or even more, but in winter it can easily be below zero and freezing.

Cathan and Bird were conscious of this as they drove slowly through the sand river bed, crawling their way up the track which would take them over the rock outcrop, into the valley on the other side. There was still half an hour's driving to do before it was completely dark.

Progress was slow. Cathan engaged the Landrover in its lowest four-wheel drive, donkey gear. He carefully maintained a slow forward speed; too fast, too slow, stalling or even rolling back could easily lead to mishap. On the downhill sections it was just the same, the Landrover kept in one gear, brakes only gently applied, if at all.

They had crossed the summit, cleared the first corner and were making their way downwards when they were forced to stop.

Standing in the middle of the track were three dusty flushed white women; two middle-aged, clearly very anxious, and a younger blonde woman who seemed slightly more composed.

'You cannot go any further,' she said, 'we have had an accident, about a hundred metres along the track. We heard your vehicle, but weren't sure you were coming our way. We were trying to get to the top of the hill to attract your attention. Please help us...please, it has been the whole day in the sun.'

Her voice wavered and her control started to fade.

'Of course,' Cathan said quietly, 'but why are you travelling alone? Is there not another vehicle with you; the golden rule in the Kaokoveld is a minimum of two cars?'

'It's a long story, we are on our own.'

The two men alighted from the Landrover. Bird let

out a low whistle at the sight facing them. A white Land Cruiser lay slewed across the track and tilted at an angle of almost 45°, along its length. The front right wheel was completely off the track, hanging freely over a sixty metre drop. Also hanging freely was the back right wheel, just off the edge of the road. The rear sump lay jammed on a large rock. It was probably this that had prevented the vehicle from somersaulting down a slope of boulders and scree.

'The rock saved them,' Bird muttered, 'only because it was not their time to die.'

'There is little we can do now, the light is fading quickly. The Land Cruiser seems wedged firmly; we will tackle the problem tomorrow.'

Cathan turned to the three women.

'I'm afraid you will have to leave everything here, taking anything off the car might just upset its balance. I have a tent and some extra bedding, we'll make camp in the riverbed at the bottom of the hill. Our vehicle will also remain here. It's too dangerous to reverse back so we'll unload as much as we need for tonight and carry it down.'

★★★

Somehow there had been no introductions, or any explanation as to why three women were travelling alone in such an isolated and remote area.

The women erected the tent whilst Bird collected wood for the fire. Cathan went back up to the Land Cruiser. As a precaution he passed a rope around its front axle securing it to another large boulder at the side of the track. He drove his vehicle closer, loosened the winch cable on the bumper, fastened it around the rear axle of the stricken vehicle, packed more stones against all the tyres and made sure that both cars were in gear with handbrakes pulled up tight.

By the time he returned, everyone had already eaten. The older women were in the tent. On the far side of the fire Bird was asleep, curled up in a kaross.

'My name is Kara,' she said softly, 'the older lady who was driving is Beth. She is the matron at the hospital where I work and the other woman is Susan, her long time companion. Not what you may think, they are two spinsters who enjoy each other's friendship and loyalty. We may appear to have been ungracious, but we are sunburnt and dehydrated. And so frightened and worried. I don't know what we would have done if you hadn't come along. I am sorry that you have been put to so much trouble.'

He looked at her. 'It will be a long, difficult day tomorrow. May have to stay overnight again. We have plenty of food and water. There is no need to be afraid. While I eat tell me what happened.'

His directness unsettled her for a moment; not in an accusing way, but more searching and scrutinising seeming to pierce her innermost being.

'We were travelling in convoy with another couple, work-colleagues of Susan, but they damaged their fuel tank. When we arrived in Palmwag to stop over and re-fuel, it was leaking badly. The ranger there said that he could find somebody to fix it, a local farmer who was also a coded welder. It might take a day or so to contact him. This was the only option, the only solution.'

She paused. Then went on.

'We discussed this between ourselves. Beth and Susan wanted to press on along our original route through the Western Kaokoveld, leaving the other two to have their fuel tank fixed. Once this was done the other couple would proceed along the better eastern road to Ruacana, then on to Epupa Falls where we would all meet up again. I felt that we should all stay together, but in the end was persuaded by Beth to join them.'

The campfire shone off her face as she continued.

'This was just the wrong thing to do. We found our way to Sesfontein all right, the road being in a reasonable condition. But when we turned onto the track leading down the Hoanib river, everything changed. What a nightmare! It took the whole day to travel fifty kilometres, the sand was so soft, and the dust!'

'It's a fine chalk dust, I am surprised you got through at all without your vehicle overheating or radiator choking,' he said.

'When we reached the Skeleton Coast Park border sign, we turned right up another track and camped there that night, still at the edge of the river. I was really scared; couldn't sleep. During the night I could have sworn that there were lions roaring in the distance - probably just my imagination.'

'I don't think so. There are lions that move from the Etosha Park, down the Hoanib, even into the Uniab riverbed as well, right to the Skeleton Coast. I have regularly seen their tracks, some years ago Bird saw one right on the beach.' He watched her as he spoke, 'they are there all right.'

In profile he saw that she was very lovely; straight fine boned nose and high cheekbones. An expressive mouth revealing an obviously chipped front tooth, full lower lip. A clear long scar ran angled down her chin.

She had managed to wash her face and brush her hair out. A lustrous golden blonde with dark undertones, it hung to her shoulders. Her eyebrows were also dark, emphasizing light blue eyes. In the depths of them, he detected an inner pain, an insecurity. Whether it was the situation she found herself in now, which he doubted, or something else, he sensed that she had suffered deeply in her life. But it was her pure complexion and skin colour that intrigued him, an imperceptible olive that reflected in the firelight.

He was busy now, selecting thick straight logs from the firewood that Bird had stacked. With a small hand axe he lopped off the thorns and spikes, stripping the loose bark away.

'What are you doing?' she asked.

'These will be used to build a supporting ramp under the back wheel so that we can lift the rear sump off the rock. Until we do that, there is no way we can consider trying to move your car.'

She watched him as he whittled the logs to size, his strong hands managing the task with ease. And then her eyes closed, the stress of the day overcoming her. Kara felt herself being gently lifted and helped into a sleeping bag. A sleeping bag that smelt of travel dust, wood smoke and male sweat.

Sometime during the early dark hours she opened her eyes. Momentarily startled, she saw that Cathan was sitting next to her, writing in what looked to be a battered diary. He turned, whispered that she was safe – the reassurance soothing in the low firelight. She fell asleep again, with a feeling of protection possessing her the like of which she had never felt before.

In the morning when she awoke the men were gone. It was early, the stillness disturbed only by the fluting chirps of a mountain chat.

An hour later the three women, carrying coffee and fruit, walked back up the track to join Cathan and Bird. Both vehicles were still in the same position, but the rear wheel of the Land Cruiser was now propped on a cantilever built with rocks and logs.

'We are going to jack it up a little, prop more stones under the rear wheel and continue to do this until we can free the sump,' Cathan explained. 'If either of the vehicles slip, we could lose them both down the slope.'

It was painstaking and backbreaking work. There was no respite from the heat; on the open hill top the sun bore down relentlessly. Helping where they could, Kara, Beth and Susan carried rocks, passed logs and moved the loose material away. At noon, Cathan sent them back down to the campsite to wait in the shade. 'Bird and I can tolerate the heat; when it gets a bit cooler, come up and help us some more.'

Some three hours later while the women were still resting, Cathan felt that the Land Cruiser was secure enough to move.

He got in and started it, engaged four wheel drive,

and with Bird operating the winch on the other vehicle, they dragged the Land Cruiser inch by inch nearer to safety.

Once they had the rear wheel securely on the track, Bird slowly reversed the Land Rover, towing the Land Cruiser on the winch cable. There was a wavering moment as the front wheel hooked on the rocky edge; then with a jolt and tyres screaming, the vehicle was safely back on the track.

Around the fire that night they discussed what the ladies should do in continuing their journey.

'My patrol route was planned for the next seven days, which would take us through the western Kaokoveld and back to my camp at Swartbooisdrift. However, you cannot travel on your own, the roads are treacherous. In some places just rocky tracks, worse than those you have just experienced.'

'How far is Epupa, where we are due to meet up with our friends?' Beth asked.

'About three full days' driving from here.'

'Three days!' The women were clearly dismayed. 'But its only about one hundred and fifty kilometres or so. What about our friends, they should be nearly there already!'

'You will only be able to do about fifty kilometers a day, and that's assuming all goes well. If you have a breakdown or puncture, or have to help someone else, add another day.'

There was silence as they all pondered the problem. In the end it was Cathan who made the decision.

'We will all travel by another track directly to my

camp at Swartbooisdrift. If your friends have made it to Epupa, on the way back they should pass us en route to the northern tarred road. Then you can join up again.'

'What if they haven't?' Beth asked.

'Then Bird and I will accompany you to the tarred road.'

Kara looked at him. 'We will do as you say,' she said simply. 'You have rescued us, how can we ever thank you.'

They were alone again as the flames danced; cicada shrilling in the night air around them. On the other side of the hearth Bird, eyes half closed, sat contemplating Cathan and Kara. A fractional smile hovered on his face, but he did not say anything. They listened to the night sounds. A deep grunting noise started behind them.

'Hu-hu-hu, hu-hu-hu.'

'What is that?' she queried.

'It's a giant eagle owl, a male,' Cathan replied. 'Listen carefully.'

A little further away a long drawn out whistling sound responded.

'That's the female.'

They sat there quietly, the large birds' calls resonating in the night air.

He looked at her in the firelight. 'What do you do at the hospital? You know, where Beth works.'

'I'm a doctor,' she replied, 'or really almost a doctor. My internship will be finished in four months' time. What a hard slog it has been, no social life, no sport, just work and study, work and study!'

Slowly her life's history came pouring out. He listened,

asked the odd question; she opened to him, talked in a way that she had never done to anyone else before. Enquiring gently, he said softly that he felt that she had experienced some difficult times. He hoped that he was not prying.

Abandoned as a baby, she spent the first twelve years of her life in an orphanage. An orphanage for coloured children. Children of mixed parentage, born out of wedlock. Born to mothers who were shamed by their communities or too poor and humble to cope. Where black communities with extended families try to rally around children; the youth she found herself in the midst of, were truly deserted. Difficult years in shabby clothes, eating poor food, beaten by the bigger children, treated like an abused animal, living without hope.

The matron and her husband ran the orphanage with brutal hands.

'They gave us no love at all. We were beaten for the most minor reasons!'

'The matron's husband would molest the older girls; I managed to evade him, till he grabbed me one day after hockey practice. When he tore my blouse I tripped him with the hockey stick. As he got up he hit me. In the face, see this scar and tooth. Some of the older girls came to help me, luckily just in time. He just went off laughing. Shortly after that I was able to leave that dreadful place.'

Her fortunes changed. A middle-aged school teacher saw an intelligence in a lost child that others had not; a kindly single woman who became her foster mother.

'Aunt Esme helped me through high school. Taught me how to speak properly, paid my university fees, has supported me for the last eleven years. She saved my life. On top of that she is totally undemanding, just a wonderful caring person. I adore her.'

Kara watched as he roasted their coffee with an ember from the fire. His quiet demeanour and total self confidence in what she observed him doing, as well as the stress of the last few days, encouraged her loquacity. She spoke of their journey so far; the tensions that arose in the touring group between individuals who did not know one another well enough. Tolerance was difficult to maintain.

'Susan and Beth have pulled themselves to one side, as you can see,' she said.

'They feel guilty for the situation you find yourselves in,' Cathan replied, 'and probably worrying about the other group as well.'

Late into the night they talked, she doing most of it, prompted by little observations from him.

'I feel so safe with you,' Kara murmured, virtually unaware that she had spoken.

He looked at her, remained quiet, sparks of the fire epitomising the scintilla that were flickering between them.

He knew it; she knew it.

★★★

It took two days to reach the road that went down to his camp.

Following on behind, Bird had taken the wheel of the other vehicle, leaving Kara to share the cab with Cathan as he led the way along the difficult tracks.

Almost subconsciously she sat close to him, often lightly resting her right hand on his knee as he drove.

The first time she did it surprised him. She almost guiltily went to remove it, but then he put his hand on hers to hold it there.

'Its been such a long time,' he said softly.

She knew what he meant and her heart soared.

***

They stopped at the junction to talk about the situation again.

Cathan pointed. 'Left takes us down to Epupa, about a day's drive. If we follow the right-hand track we should reach my camp in about four hours.'

Bird held up his arm. 'There is a car coming, it is alone.'

At first the others could not hear anything, but he was right. A trail of fawn-grey dust gradually drew nearer. Twenty minutes later a vehicle came into view.

'It is our friends,' Beth exclaimed, 'they must have been delayed.'

Cathan and Bird stood to one side as the group gathered around discussing the last five days' occurrences. Eventually they all came over to the two men.

Beth was the spokesperson. 'We are very grateful for your help, to both of you,' she said, 'but we would like to push on to Epupa, especially now that we are all together again.'

'It's a beautiful place,' Cathan affirmed with a little grin. 'The track has recently been graded. If you drive carefully and slowly, you should be fine.'

'We'll stop at your camp on the way back, just to let you know that everything is all right,' Beth stated.

Just as Cathan started his vehicle to drive off, Kara ran over to him.

'All but me. I would like to stay with you, that is, if you would like me to… will… allow me to.'

He looked at her, not answering.

It was Bird who replied. 'Ag, he is too shy, Missie, you are welcome. I will look after you.'

And he laughed, an infectious caring laugh, with a toothy smile that revealed his fondness for the white man, and his appreciation for the situation.

★★★

Kara was surprised when she saw his base camp on the banks of the Kunene River.

'How long have you lived here?' she asked.

'Just over four years,' Cathan replied.

It was a pleasing orderly place. The old building, now home and office, was neatly painted in a light beige to match the surroundings. Hanging over the window openings were roll-down awnings made with reeds. Shade netting had been stretched across the roof to provide more cover and coolness.

Neatly tucked away in an enclosure of trees was another small, newly built structure of poles and thatch.

'This is the bathroom,' he said, 'always look carefully before you use it, sometimes there's a mouse or spider lurking in a corner. If you want hot water,

Bird will fire up the boiler.'

'You have electricity, here?' she queried.

'No, no...its just a 44 gallon drum filled with water, under which we make a fire. There is a relief valve to let off the steam. Works really well, though.'

She held his hand as they walked, taking pleasure in the evident pride he took in showing her around. Under the tall palm trees a garden had been laid out; an attractive area divided into flower beds, vegetable patch and a small lawn of thick bladed grass.

Cathan led her down to the Kunene.

'Water is pumped to the house from here,' he said, pointing to a pipe leading into the slow flowing river. 'If the rains are good in Angola, we have to be careful, we could easily lose our pump and equipment.'

'What about crocodiles?' Kara asked.

'In this stretch there aren't any, it's very shallow. But there are crocs further up and down stream where it's deeper. In fact, most times it's so low here that vehicles can easily cross into Angola. Very occasionally the police or customs people will use it.'

'This is such a beautiful place,' she said lifting her face to him. And Kara kissed him softly, an ephemeral touch on the side of his face. He lifted his arm to her shoulders as the late afternoon sun cast rubescent light across the languid water.

The two of them were alone that evening.

'Bird lives with a local woman,' Cathan told her. 'She was originally part of a nomadic group, but the two of them have now built a hut and kraal not far away, just up the river. Sometimes they join me here in the evenings, if they think I've been on my own too long. Worried about me going bush mad.'

Kara watched him, his rangy frame bent as he stoked the fire. Earlier when she had just finished showering and was returning to the house, she saw him washing down at the river. From the rear his nudity was provocative, darkly tanned except for the area normally covered by his shorts. He was lean and strong; she hoped almost contritely, that he would turn around to face her.

A saying of Aunt Esme's came to her, 'Tensile steel does not need to be thick,' and she giggled out aloud.

Cathan turned to her, smiling, 'Private joke?'

'Mmm...yes.'

Quietly they sat there as the night drew in. She gripped his left arm tightly.

'Cathan, I must ask and you know why I'm asking. Are you married or do you have a girlfriend?' Words that were stilted, half blurted, as if Kara was scared of finding out.

He looked at her, felt her apprehension.

'I have no-one.' A meditative pause. 'There was a woman a long time ago, but it didn't, couldn't work out.'

Kara drew a deep breath. Turning in her chair to look at him, she leaned forward; saw his face solemn and thoughtful.

'I have no-one either. I went out with a boy at university for a while. He only wanted one thing then it was over.'

Cathan put his arms around her. Into his ear she breathed, 'I'm in love with you.'

For a long time they sat there. Slowly the logs burnt down. The night grew colder and as the flames died, he held her.

'Kara, I'm falling too, I can't believe it.'

They walked to his house, arms wrapped around each other. She did not want to let go but he was firm.

'I'll sleep on the camp bed in my office, you use the bedroom.'

'Share the bed with me,' she whispered.

'Soon, not yet.' He embraced her and then their first kiss, yearning, deep, exultant and arousing. Gently he pulled away.

***

'You will need to read these,' he quietly said the next morning, 'this is what I could not tell you yesterday. Even after all this time I still feel guilty. Or perhaps not guilty in the deepest sense of the word, in the sense that I was fully responsible for Leigh-Ann's actions, but guilty in the knowledge that I knew she would have emotional problems. But it's probably the sadness that gets to me; the hurt and distress she went through. I should have done more.'

He touched her cheek softly, 'I will be in the workshop repairing the Landrover's gearbox.'

With some apprehension she opened the envelope and unfolded the letters, which were creased and had obviously been read many times. There was still something in the envelope which she left there; a small object of sorts. Not knowing what to expect, she found that her hands were shaking slightly, her heart seemed to be beating more quickly, almost unevenly.

The letters appeared to be in a particular order and she began to read.

Monday, ________

My dear Cathan,

It is sad news that I bring you. Leigh Ann died last Friday and was cremated as per her wishes yesterday.

Also in accordance with her wishes, I have enclosed her ashes. Her request to me was that she wanted you to bury her in a special place to you, in the knowledge that you would be her final guardian and the most important person ever to have been in her life.

My son, do not think that this is macabre and grim, but consider it more a gift of great love and respect. Bury her in that special place, knowing that she is now at peace.

As I sat her bedside, her very last words before she lapsed into coma - words that did not really make sense to me, were,

'tell Cathan, I am running before that wind'.

She passed away an hour later.

I feel very heart sore for you and grieve for Leigh Ann; I had a closeness to her, as if she were a long lost sister, and now in hindsight regret that I never did enough for her. I should have stayed in touch with her regularly.

Your ever loving mother,

____

Drawing her breath deeply she opened the next one.

St Vincents
Daughters of Charity
Hospice and Sanatorium
Rustenberg
South Africa

Dear Mr _____

I am writing to bring you news of a person you know as Mrs Leigh Ann Robinson, but whom we call Sister Ann.

Some four years ago, she visited us, saying that she represented a potential donor and had come to see our facilities and staffing and to determine what our financial resources were. I showed her around; she could see that we were significantly under funded and short staffed. Our Hospice looks after the terminally infirm and destitute, victims of physical and sexual abuse, across all the population sectors and all age groups. We are inundated with patients.

She returned two days later. In my office that morning, she said that she had brought the donation, but before handing it over, there were two conditions attached to the donation that she hoped I would understand and agree to.

The conditions were not that difficult. Firstly she wanted to live at the Hospice for the rest of her life and work for us on a full-time basis without remuneration. The board and lodging would be sufficient reward. Her second stipulation was in the event of something untoward happening to her, or her death, I was to forward the enclosed envelope, and a small locket that she was wearing, to you. That was all.

I explained to her that the life we lead is very austere, subject to long hours, hard work and many disappointments. But she told me that she had considered this very carefully and that all she had left in her life was the capacity to work hard.

Mr _______, the decision I had to make was not all that onerous. She was sincere in her requests, the Hospice is always short staffed and the cheque she had brought, made out to us and bank guaranteed, was for well over one million rands.

She arrived that day and has been with us ever since. Some eighteen months after her arrival Sister Ann appeared to have a total nervous breakdown, became cataleptic and would not leave her room. Nobody could get through to her. We all tried; I even managed to get a psychiatrist, a psychoanalyst and priests to visit her, but all was in vain. As a last resort, I looked up the address on the envelope she had left for you, obtained the telephone number from our local exchange and tried to contact you. The lady who answered my call and whom I now know is your mother explained that you were far away, beyond contact and would be so for the foreseeable future.

Your mother asked me why I wanted to contact you so urgently and I told her of the predicament I was facing with Sister Ann.

Your mother was quiet for a moment. Then said that she had some insight into the problem, and that she would come up to us the next weekend and spend some time with Ann.

She spent two days in the room with Ann, emerging only to refresh herself shortly and to get some tea and toast for both of them. On the Sunday evening, your mother and Ann came to me in my office whereupon your mother told me that Ann was now ready to return to work.

I do not know what your mother said or did, or even if she has told you of these events, but Ann returned to work, even more industriously than before. She never seems to sleep or rest, just pushes herself relentlessly.

There was, however, one very significant difference. She has never spoken again, not a single sound or noise. She helps our patients with gestures and her own limited version of sign language.

I have digressed somewhat in this letter to you, but have tried to put matters into context.

You will recall that Sister Ann's second condition, when joining us, had been that in the event of something untoward happening to her, I was to forward the envelope addressed to you, plus the small locket.

I fear that the 'untoward' is now.

In the four years that she has been here, Ann has left our premises only once. That was two weeks ago, when a few of us went to a symphony concert at the local town hall. It had been a surprise to all when she decided to join us. We were so hoping that this was a step to her recovering her speech and easing up on herself. During the performance of one of Mozart's beautiful quartets, I noticed that she was openly crying and we all tried to comfort her. To no avail.

She no longer eats, drinks only a little water from time to time, never sleeps and yet still tries to work as hard as ever. She is becoming weaker by the day and has already collapsed on several occasions. After her last collapse, without a noise or gesture, she handed the locket to me, which I have included with these letters.

I believe that she has lost her remaining will to live and a sad day faces us all shortly.

Your mother has been informed and she is visiting us again next week; she has promised to try and contact you in the meantime.

I am sure that the news in my letter will be distressing to you, but Sister Ann has chosen her path. She has made a tremendous contribution and been a wonderful asset to our institution.

The Lord God will now protect her and give her peace.

Yours Sincerely

Reverend Mother Marie-Louise

By the end of the second letter, tears were streaming down her cheeks. Kara gathered herself before opening the third; the contents of sadness and despair were almost too overwhelming for her to read on.

Darling,

I Love You.

You once said to me that people, events and education shape our lives, but that very small destinies truly change our lives. That our two dogs were destined to chase each other, that day on the beach, changed my life forever.

When Jack returned from Australia, I asked him for a divorce. I re-assured him that it was through no fault of his. I was happy to leave the marriage without anything. No assets or possessions, no money. I did not tell him why, he was shocked enough and I did not want to hurt him anymore.

You see, knowing that I was unfaithful was wrong, but as you taught me in that short time we were together, integrity and honesty are the most important personal attributes to have and display.

I had come to realise that, to stay married to Jack, but to always love you, was not being fair or decent towards him. I am determined to live the remainder of my life in as honest a way as I can.

We wound up our marriage, Jack was very generous to me, to the extent of settling one and half million rands into my bank account.

I met yesterday with a Mother Superior who runs a Catholic Hospice and have decided to donate all my money to it, on the condition that I can live and work there. I am sure that she will accept this, as she seems to be desperate for funds and staff. I have investigated various institutions to help, but the one I have chosen is where, I believe, I can contribute the most.

I know that you will approve.

I also know that I am in deep emotional trouble. Not a moment passes, ***not a moment*** *when I do not think of you; of what we shared and did and of wondering what you may be doing now.*

Everything is recalled as if it were here and now, or even just yesterday.

Your loss to me is like a gaping wound with blood flowing freely, unable to be staunched.

I have contemplated so many things, religious order, emigration, travel, coming to live near you, asking you to marry me, even suicide – all these are wrong, you are twenty five years younger than me, your life lies ahead, I must stand alone.

I know that you said that if I was in any distress or faced major problems, you would come to me immediately. I know you meant this and would do it and I love you even more for it. But no, that is not right or fair, you must develop your life, do the important things that will help others – let many more than just I, have access to you.

I wish that we could have lived and shared a lifetime together, but that was not to be and I am reconciled to the fact that I will never see you again.

My darling Cathan, this letter will reach you when I am at the end of my existence. Have no remorse or regret, just remember the happiness we shared and live a long and wonderfully rewarding life.

Yours, forever

Leigh Ann

Deeply distressed by what she had read, Kara studied the letters again, opened the locket, saw the two names linked. These little acts, together with the compassion that was flowing through her, seemed to exhaust her strength.

She sat there wondering what to do. She had told Cathan that she was falling in love with him; Cathan had said to her that he was developing strong feelings for her and, to be fair on him, he had not concealed anything. But somehow everything had taken on a new light. A light that was clouded with Leigh-Ann's death and, as she now realised, her own sense of jealousy and envy.

Bird was working in the vegetable garden, carefully weeding between the plants when she joined him. He greeted her but Kara was still overcome. They worked together in the heat and she took solace in the coloured man's company. She helped him stake the runner beans and vine tomatoes; together they carefully checked the heads of the lettuces and cabbages.

'Now you know his pain Missie', Bird murmured, 'it is a big thing he carries on his back, his load is heavy.'

'Do you know the story, Bird?' she asked.

'No, Missie, I only know where the grave is.'

'You know where the grave is?'

'Yes, Missie, it is far from here. I helped him make the cross. I said the prayer when we were finished. I must go and pump water now'.

And then Kara was alone, brooding and miserable, sad and confused.

That she was in love with Cathan was beyond doubt. That she was jealous of his previous relationship was certain. But Leigh Ann was dead and Cathan must have suffered terribly; both in the knowledge of her death and in finalising her last wishes. And then the envy crept in again. Where were Leigh Ann's remains buried and would Cathan really love her? Would he be able to love only her and not make comparisons between the two of them.

'I can't walk away from this,' Kara muttered to herself.

'I love this man…and this place.'

In her mind she had already worked it out. She wanted to finalise her internship and then return to Cathan to live in the Koakoveld, work with him and apply her medical training to help the local people.

But was Cathan capable of loving her, loving her with intensity, despite his relationship with Leigh Ann? Was it too much to expect of him? Can one love for the second time?

All these thoughts and more swirled around in her head, what to do, what to say, what lay ahead, should she go home, never see him again, try and get over him, move on.

★★★

There was an air of tension as the three of them sat

around the fire that evening. Even the dog sensed the unease and lay in the shadows beyond the flickering light and not, as usual, close to Cathan at his feet.

Few words were exchanged. Cathan gazed pensively at the fire and Kara was picking at some needlework, mending a pair of her slacks. Bird was sucking at an unlit pipe, which he removed and put in his shirt pocket.

Then quietly he began to speak.

'Near the beginning, before the Creator had made man, when the sky and the earth and the elements were in harmony; the Morning Star, the most brilliant light in the sky, decided to take a wife.

He considered all the animals for a suitable mate. It was a difficult decision; animals were plentiful, there were many splendid creatures to consider. Eventually he narrowed his selection down to the cat family.

Morning Star rejected the regal lioness for being too large and aggressive, the nocturnal leopard was too furtive and dangerous, the cheetah too timid.

In a clearing near a waterhole he built a hut and then he made his choice.

Morning Star chose a partner; a beautiful lynx, a red cat of sleek and slender shape.'

'But why a lynx?' Kara murmured, sewing set aside.

'If you observe the lynx in the veld,' Bird continued, 'you will see that it is a lovely animal. Gleaming russet red fur and a handsome face. Sculpted tufted ears, black markings up to the eyes, white surrounds to the eyelids, white under the chin. A really beautiful being. And with its beauty comes more. It's brave and strong, fiercely protective of its family and home, a good provider to her little ones, a loving mother and guardian.'

'But matters changed for the worse. Female Hyena came to hear that Morning Star had selected Lynx to be his wife. Female Hyena was beside herself with jealousy, how could she not have been chosen?

She and her brothers waited until Lynx had moved into the hut that Morning Star had built for her, and there they kept her prisoner. Day and night they barricaded the doorway, not allowing her the freedom to hunt or drink.

Lynx became thinner and weaker every day.

It was Lynx's sister who told Morning Star what had happened. He was livid; down to Earth he streaked and set about the loitering hyena pack. They scattered in all directions, screeching and howling. Female Hyena took such fright and ran straight through the fire. Burnt and maimed, she limped off into the night – the markings and deformity hyena bear to this day.

Morning Star was reconciled with Lynx; harmony was restored.'

'Oh Bird, that is such a wonderful story,' Kara exclaimed, tears in her eyes as she went over to the little man and hugged him.

'Missie, the bushmen know how things work.'

Turning, she saw Cathan looking at her, saw the affection in his face, saw something more. The reserve was lifted, a burden gone.

'How you must have grieved, and the blame. What you both must have suffered.' Kara took his hand to her face, lifted it to her lips.

'I love you,' she said, 'and I trust you.'

There was a quiet cough. Bird said goodnight, disappearing off into the night, to his own little home in the bush.

Cathan fetched his groundsheet and sleeping bag from the house; spread them on the soft ground near the fire. They held each other in the warmth of his bedding, surrounded by the cool silent night. She slid her arm inside his shirt, felt the strength of his shoulders; fell asleep in the comfort of his arms.

Entwined they lay together. Cathan could not sleep. Throughout the night he held Kara, listening to her steady breathing; through her clothes he perceived how peaceful she was in repose.

He could not believe what was happening. Almost out of nowhere, this young, intelligent, slightly vulnerable woman was in his life. The suddenness of it all; it had been just six days. His solitude these last years was dispersing with every breath she took next to him.

That he had done so much was not in doubt. In the time he had lived here, his doctorate was completed. Research papers and reports on desert elephants were in circulation; another language mastered. Based on the quality of his work, he was becoming recognised as an authority on the Kaokoveld.

There had been interaction with others, but in such a remote area, with limited communication, it had all been very difficult and irregular.

The profound affect of Leigh Ann's death, even though her letter had tried to console him. But now Kara was here. His heart and mind exalted.

***

'What are we going to do today?' she asked, as they

sat eating their breakfast on the terrace next to his house.

'I'm taking the day off, we're going on a little boat trip,' he said with an enigmatic smile, 'Bird will soon be here to help us.'

'What must I wear?'

'Your swimming costume, shorts and a hat. You may need a long-sleeved shirt as well, protection against the sun. Oh ... and wear your walking shoes.'

An hour later they were driving along the river's edge on a stony gravel track. Early on the air was crisp. By the time they reached their destination, the temperature had steadily risen to over 20° Celsius. Cathan stopped the vehicle near a rocky promontory.

Kara could see the river to her right; when she looked the other way there was nothing. She wanted to say something, but the two men were already busy. From the back of the Landrover they unloaded a bulky half-inflated vessel.

'What is that?' she queried.

'It's a two man white water raft.'

A foot-pump was produced, which Bird used to fully inflate the raft. Oars were secured within the rope-lines. A small plastic cool box placed in a water-tight compartment.

Cathan and Bird lifted the raft onto their shoulders and made their way around the outcrop. Now Kara realised that they were at the top of a waterfall, with a series of rapids trailing down to her left.

Cathan turned to her. 'This is the Ondoruso gorge.'

'We're not going in there?' Kara wavered, pointing to the fast white plume of water, which dropped twenty metres into a rock-strewn pool.

'No, we'll portage around it and start lower.'

A small sandy beach, on a bend where the river slowed, was the starting point. Bird left them there, returning to the vehicle; he arranged to meet them down the river later in the day.

'Put this on,' Cathan said, handing over a yellow life-jacket, 'we are ready to go!'

'Cathan, what must I do, I'm getting scared.'

'Just hold onto the lead rope, keep the nose up high. I'll paddle and steer.'

'What happens if we capsize?'

'Float downstream with your legs up until you find a rock you can hold on to.'

'And crocodiles?'

'None here, not in the rapids, further along maybe, in the open flatter water.'

They negotiated the first descent fairly easily, Cathan navigating the raft expertly between the rocks.

'The next one is the most difficult. There is a small whirlpool at the bottom. Hold on tight!'

'I suppose it has a name,' she shouted above the sound of the wild water.

'Devil's pothole,' he called back.

'I just knew it!'

The charge of it took her breath away. Over the edge they flew down into the white churning water below. For a moment, the vortex sucked them in. Cathan paddled furiously. Then they were free, albeit going backwards, hitting boulders on either side until he could straighten the raft out.

For an hour they sped on, one small cataract after the next; the spray in their faces, the exhilaration of not being fully in control, the stark remoteness of the area. No other people around.

At the bottom of the gorge where the river flattened out he paddled over to a fallen tree, which had a large branch lying in the water. Fastening the rope around it, he turned to her, 'we can take off the life jackets now and bail out.' The raft was filled with water a third deep.

'From here on we'll just float on to where Bird is waiting for us.'

Drifting downstream in the brilliant late morning sunlight, Kara lay stretched out across the width of the raft, her head propped up on one side, legs raised on the other. She felt drowsy, the rushing danger and excitement over.

Looking at him through half closed eyes, she could see that he too was relaxed; Cathan guiding the raft with small sweeps of his paddle.

'What are you thinking of?' she murmured.

'It's a serious thought. Have you ever tried to find out who your parents were?'

'I have wondered, but the struggle to survive in that terrible orphanage was greater than a yearning to know. When I was younger, before Aunt Esme took me in, there was a time when it worried me. She offered to help me to try and find them; by then I wasn't really interested.'

'Aunt Esme thinks my mother must have been white, perhaps from Europe, Nordic; and my father a Malay from the Cape. But it's all conjecture. I have her and now I've met you.'

The current carried them on. Kara had stripped to a

low-cut swimsuit, her body lithe and slim, skin a natural aureate olive in the sunlight.

He looked as she dozed. She was stunning and unspoilt, unaffected by her attractiveness and intelligence. Rotating slightly to one side, her left breast fell free, the exposed nipple small and dark brown. Cathan wanted to lean forward and touch her, his arousal intensified by her innate beauty.

But he held back and turned his attention to the birdlife and surroundings. A pied kingfisher caught his eye; the black and white bird hovering over the water before plunge-diving in to seize its prey. Further on, a large crocodile slipped into the river and disappeared from view.

Around the next bend, Bird was waiting for them in a clearing on the riverbank.

Quietly Cathan called her, 'we are here now, you'll have to wake up.' Kara stretched, unselfconsciously gathering herself together.

'It's so peaceful. I feel so good.' She leaned over and kissed him, a deep searching kiss of love and burgeoning passion.

'How many days do you have left, before you go back to work?'

'Another ten days, why?'

'I need to go to Windhoek for a seminar, could take you there. On the way I would like to show you something.'

'What?' she asked.

'There is an elephant group that I have been observing for some years now, we could try and find them as we travel down.'

'I'd love to do that, to see desert elephants. I've read about them of course. But to see them would be wonderful. Elephants are such marvellous creatures.'

'It's quite a trip. No guarantee we'll find them,' Cathan said.

'I know, but let's try,' she said eagerly.

He smiled and agreed.

★★★

Cathan and Kara drove steadily, leaving Swartbooisdrift well before sunrise making their way past Epembe on to Opuwo, the administrative town for the region. Stocking up, they turned left, heading down a stony track towards the tiny settlement of Orupembe.

At Orupembe, after fourteen hours in the Landrover covering just on three hundred kilometres, they stopped in the Khumib, a dry sand river, to overnight.

Kara looked at Cathan as he grilled their meat on the fire. Even after such an arduous day, he appeared unruffled and strong. She was exhausted.

Even Bird looked tired, lying slumped on his blankets.

'That was a long day, my love,' she said, 'how far tomorrow?'

'We'll follow this watercourse for a few hours until we hit the road to Purros. Then its about fifty kilometres.'

'Are we going to camp there?'

'Yes, maybe spend two or three nights. See if the elephants are in the area.'

The tiny Himba settlement was almost deserted when they arrived. Lean, small pale dogs lay in the shade. A few women sat outside their huts, either watching their little children playing in the dust or with babies suckling.

'The men are far way, maybe three days,' Bird stated after talking to them.

'Ask them about the elephants,' Kara requested excitedly.

'I have, the people haven't seen them for more than two months.'

Her face dropped. She looked disappointed.

'But I think they are on the way,' the little man said.

'How can you tell?'

Bird shrugged his shoulders; looked eastwards, said nothing more.

Pitching tents under a great jutting overhanging rock they set up camp.

Normally Cathan would sleep under the stars, but it was cold at the side of the Hoarusib river. The winter weather was clear and crisp; the nights outdoors freezing.

Kara was surprised that the river was flowing. Shallow crystal clear water in a slow narrow stream.

'There is always water here,' Cathan said, 'even if there has been very little rain.'

Leaving Bird at the campsite they drove down river a little way, to a pool where they could wash and change into clean clothes.

He filled a bucket with water and gave it to her.

'Oh, I'll just splash in the pool,' she said.

'I don't think so,' he replied.

'Why not?'

'Just put your foot in then you'll see.'

Puzzled, she stood for a moment, then did as he said.

Within a minute, she squealed. Looking down she saw something had bitten her.

'What is it?

'Watch,' he said, 'I did try to warn you.'

'But it's so sore!'

He pulled the leech off, already swollen with her blood to the size of a large coin.

She looked at the parasite as he held it between his fingers.

'I can't believe that doctors used these for blood letting and to reduce fevers,' she said, 'can you just imagine it.'

'That's why you have to be careful.'

Refreshed they walked up stream a while, until he stopped. Sitting on a large rock a little distance from the river, the afternoon breeze blew softly, intermittently, into their faces.

'This is a good spot. Look through the binoculars; you can see a long way up the watercourse. I've often seen animals from here!'

'Elephants?'

'Yes, but others too, zebra and springbok. And some interesting birds.'

But it was quiet and still. Little stirred or moved. The land, the environment seemed to be in dreamlike limbo, the gentle, gusting wind a passive soothing sound.

★★★

The next morning they set out once more. This time Bird went with them. Hiking further along to a better, higher vantage point and overlooking a large pool surrounded by reeds and scrub, they waited. Cathan was reading and Kara dozing in the sun when three hours later Bird moved, stood up slowly. He nodded, pointing northwards. Cathan touched Kara's arm.

The three of them knelt behind a boulder looking in the direction Bird had indicated. The first sign was small dust cloud; some birds took off suddenly, then quietude again.

Kara looked, not seeing anything.

Bird spoke softly, 'Meme is here.'

'Who?' she asked.

Cathan smiled, 'wait and see.'

Slowly and in single file, the elephants ranged into view. The big matriarch in front, followed by four more, then the last two, a shambling male shepherded along by a large female. For a while the matriarch had her trunk up. Then she lowered, it turning her body in their direction.

'Meme knows we're here, we can go closer now,' Cathan said.

'Aren't we close enough?' Kara was anxious.

He took her hand. Cautiously they approached the animals grouped around the water.

'They trust us, we must trust them,' he whispered.

The seven elephants seemed to be totally relaxed in the presence of Bird, Kara and Cathan. They drank steadily from the pool, throwing water up and over themselves, slurping and splashing. Mud sprayed and solidified on their great bodies, gentle noises of contentment rumbled.

Bird and Cathan noticed it at the same time.

'Nightingale is pregnant,' the white man whispered.

'Who is Nightingale?' Kara could hardly keep her voice low. She was shaking with barely contained tension.

'The large elephant standing next to the male.'

'We call her that after Florence Nightingale. She cares for the one next to her. We've named him Bullit.'

'How do you know that?'

'Know what?'

'That she cares for him.'

'This is a female group, he's the only male. Something's happened to him, we think he's been shot, with the bullet lodged near his brain. He may now also be nearly blind.'

'How old is he?' she went on.

'Still fairly young, probably about thirty.'

'He must be the father,' Kara whispered.

'No, we've been watching him for a long time now. He's impotent, shows no sexual awareness at all. He eats, drinks, a little play with the youngest ones. But he's fit and strong, protected within the group.'

'Isn't it just so wonderful, isn't it wonderful.' Kara could hardly hold back her excitement.

***

They were making love in Cathan's sleeping bag that night.

'Don't stop now, my darling, it's so good,' Kara murmured.

'Sssh, listen, we have a visitor.'

'What?'

'Sssh, listen.'

A soft purring vibration touched the night air outside the tent. There was a swish in the sand, a padding sound and then the purr again.

'It's Meme. She's checking up on us.'

'Are we safe?'

'Oh yes, it's the sound she makes of contentment. I am sure she takes pleasure from ours. I have heard her do it before, when something else has pleased her.'

And then Kara was crying softly underneath him, her tears touching his lips as the wonderment overtook her.

★★★

Parked under a camelthorn tree in the shade, Cathan and Bird waited at the edge of the airstrip for her to return.

It had been nearly four months since Kara had left to finish her qualification. The great distance and his inaccessibility made regular communication very difficult. They managed three telephone conversations; a few lovelorn letters eventually reached each other.

Cathan couldn't wait to see her again. Normally calm and controlled, he could feel his pulse chasing as he sat there.

'There will be a surprise,' Bird murmured.

'What do you mean?'

Bird was silent; then he pointed to the sky.

'The plane is bigger, not the normal one.'

Cathan looked up and around. He couldn't see or hear anything.

'It's not even here yet. What on earth are you talking about?'

'Just wait and see,' the little man said.

He was correct of course. Ten minutes later Cathan could hear the drone and slowly the aeroplane came into view. The pilot circled the strip twice, descended carefully and made a perfect landing. It was not the normal small twin-engine, but a larger one capable of carrying more than the usual two or three passengers. At the end of the runway it stopped and the two men made their way over to it.

The pilot lowered the gangway ladder and clambered down. Kara was the first to follow, waving happily to Cathan before she turned to help a matronly lady. Then consternation really kicked in. Following them were his parents, his brother and sister, and a man unknown to him. Lastly, smiling broadly, came Jan Steyn his tough, usually cynical boss from HQ. He in turn was supporting the arm of a small affectionate woman that Cathan knew to be his wife.

Cathan stood with a perplexed smile on his face as they all crowded around him. Gay and exuberant, Kara introduced him to the people he hadn't met before.

'This is my Aunt Esme,' she said.

'And you are Cathan, the one who has made my Kara so happy. And me too.' The large woman ignored his outstretched hand, pulling him to her in a comfortable embrace.

Shaking his hand, the unfamiliar man was Professor Rob Thornton, an academic theologian from the University of Cape Town.

'Will somebody please tell me what is going on?' Cathan asked.

There was a pregnant pause.

'You're getting married, old son,' Jan Steyn bellowed, 'she's got you by the short and curlies.'

'Jan, your language!' his little wife admonished.

'Ja, Ma,' and the whole group laughed.

Stunned, yet inwardly delighted, he looked around.

'What about a ring, a priest, and where are you all going to stay? Food supplies?'

Kara looked up, hugging him firmly, 'we have brought everything, even extra tents. And .... Prof Rob has agreed to marry us.'

★★★

The next evening they were married. A simple ceremony under the tall palms alongside the Kunene River. It was so out of the ordinary; everyone still and enthralled. Even the local Himba families watched with quiet respect and dignity.

Kara radiantly svelte and beautiful in a shimmering satin dress that Aunt Esme had made.

The professor conducted the formalities; vows and rings were exchanged. The small group applauded when they shared their first married kiss. When it was over the group of Himba women who were there started singing and ululating, whilst their men prepared a meat-feast a little way away. They brought beer around, made from honey and bark mixed with grass seeds harvested from ants' nests. All those there sipped from the pail.

Later on the two groups came together and the white people watched the Himba sing and dance. One of the men played tunes on a mouth bow. The women chanted and clapped. The black people moved and swayed into portrayal dances of predators and elephants and birds.

Kara was rapt; so were they all.

The night did not seem to end. But slowly, one by one everyone went to bed. The Himba drifted off into the night. Some, those that had walked in from afar, slept right next to the fire. At last the couple were on their own, sitting together. Every so often Cathan would get up to put another log on. Their great joy bound them. Arms around each other, they watched the new dawn break.

★★★

Living together so far away from a normal western way of life, their regimen unfolded to a different time frame. A Monday to Friday working system did not apply. The environment moulded their planning.

Kara, now a qualified doctor, started to establish tiny clinics in the remote villages. Sometimes it was just a makeshift shelf in a headman's hut. On Cathan's field trips they would include these clinics on his rounds. The quest for medical supplies was always a problem, but steadily she built a small stock of essentials and emergency necessities.

To cope with the demands of their nomadic lifestyle the Himba were inherently fit and strong. There was the occasional venereal disease to be treated; men who had migrated to the larger towns hundreds of kilometres away, returning back to their families once they had made a little money. So Kara's care was more for the young and old. An occasional broken bone needed setting; a sickly baby needed help, a burn wound when someone drunkenly slept too close to a fire.

She started to maintain statistics on the Himba women. Virginity was neither essential nor general; they could also be sterile for long periods of time, especially during draught and famine. Western ailments like diabetes and high blood pressure were virtually unknown.

But most of all, she enjoyed travelling with Cathan. Two weeks of journey, followed by two weeks at their base camp.

***

Kara was sure that the night she conceived was on the same day Nightingale brought her little calf to them. It just had to be.

A year had passed since they found the female elephant pregnant and now, coincidentally, were at the same pool as before. This time Kara and Cathan were returning from a short holiday at the coast when they came upon the group.

As they drove down into the riverbed the elephants were there. But this time there were nine. The group had increased by two. Not only had Nightingale given birth but there was also another young one. A calf of about six months which Meme carefully protected.

'I think she's adopted an abandoned calf,' Cathan

said, 'the matriarch sometimes does it, very occasionally, probably from a kinship group.'

But it was Nightingale who surprised them the most. She left her ward Bullit browsing some distance away. In fact it seemed to the humans that the big damaged elephant was drifting asleep.

Nightingale came towards them. Not slowly or quickly, just measuring the distance; with her tiny calf, half running, half slipping, behind in her broad shadow.

And then she stopped. Just three metres away. It was a mesmerising moment. With her great trunk Nightingale reached around and nudged the little individual forward, pushing it gently nearer to the human beings. There was a pride that would not be disguised.

'Hold out your hand,' Cathan whispered to Kara.

With her hand open, quivering slightly, fingers stretched out, Kara reached to the small animal, an almost perfect miniature of its eight ton mother. Curiosity overcame it, a graceful trunk with its tip as an extended finger touched her hand for a quick investigative caress.

Calmly, and in control of all, Nightingale's own trunk came forward guiding her baby back to her side. With a soft rumble of satisfaction she turned, mother and baby making their way back to their disabled companion. The introduction was over. The spell ended.

A bond created, reciprocation to follow.

***

Kara found her fascination with the Himba people, the women in particular. She found their self sufficiency and independence intimidating. They were always strong and healthy, even in the driest and harshest of conditions. About the only thing she could help them with was vaseline. Traditionally, the women tended to smear themselves with a mixture of butter fat, ochre and herbs. But now they seemed to prefer the clear petroleum jelly as a moisturiser, sun protector and general beauty product.

Exhausting the few books Cathan had managed to find on the Himba she found herself at a loss on what to do next; until she was befriended by Maveko. At first Kara found it difficult to determine the reason for the friendship. Maveko was younger than Kara by some six years, had never left her little village, never been to school, spoke no other language but her own.

It was Bird who explained.

'Missie, her elders say that she is a rebel, a restless one. But I think that it is more than that, Maveko is a clever one. She hungers for knowledge. She realises you have knowledge.'

Communication was not easy. Not being a linguist, Kara struggled with the Himba-Herero language. Using simple signs and the few words she had gleaned, was about all she could do. Surprisingly, Kara discovered that Maveko could grasp her questions far more quickly than she could understand Maveko's answers.

There came the time that conversation became easier.

'Tell me about your family?' Kara once questioned.

And when the answer had been fashioned, out came the return and far deeper query.

'Where is your family, why don't you all live together?'

The concept of being an orphan with no extended

family to look after one, no-one taking responsibility for a baby, was so foreign to Maveko's understanding that she checked Kara's reply out with Bird first before accepting it.

Maveko would visit Kara as often as three or four times a week. The two women would sit and talk for an hour or two and later in the evening, Kara would share the same conversation with Cathan.

'How can one live so simply, and yet be so wise?' Kara would ask him.

'There are so many things. The story-telling and oral traditions, the respect for their old people. They will always listen to their elders, even if it is something that they have heard many times before.'

He paused.

'The Himba know that life experience is knowledge to be shared. To learn from.'

When Kara told Maveko that she was pregnant, the black woman was so happy. She danced and ululated and then was suddenly gone. The next afternoon she returned, accompanied by many of the women from the surrounding area. They danced and sang and at the end, with deliberate solemnity, the oldest, who was also Maveko's widowed grandmother, presented Kara with a tiny leather loin cloth.

With a singular, rather explicit hand gesture, she indicated that Kara's yet-to-be born baby would definitely be a boy.

★★★

About a month later, Kara received the invitation to visit Maveko's homestead.

The Himba woman tried to explain. 'My father … show you fire. Sit at fire.' Maveko had no other words or signs to indicate the significance of the request.

Kara remained puzzled. Cathan thought he knew what it meant.

'For your friendship to continue, they want to introduce you to their ancestors. It's a great honour.'

'Have you been ….introduced?' Kara asked.

'Yes, but not here. Not in this area. There is a clan near Purros. I helped them when one of the men got into trouble. He was selling cattle for cheap western liquor and not telling the others. And then just after that there was another similar incident with the same man again.'

'How did you help them?'

'I suggested to the elders that he should be relocated to a familial clan that live deep in Angola. There he wouldn't be in a position to trade valuable cattle away.'

'I'm surprised the Himba didn't deal with the matter themselves. Take the law into their own hands.'

'Normally they would. But this was a much-loved son, handsome, witty and less serious, slowly succumbing to white man's alcohol. He was also unmarried which made the move easier.'

***

Kara was not sure what to expect when Maveko and Bird accompanied her to the local homestead. She had obviously been in Himba villages before but always with specific purpose: to attend children with eye infections, inject a man who had a sexually transmitted disease, discuss general health and hygiene with the women.

Now as a visitor and guest, she felt different, unconfident, a bit jittery.

They led her into the village through the entrance, then around the back of the huts, making her sit to the side of the main hut to wait for the headman.

Squatting next to her, Bird described the layout, 'in the centre, you can see the calf enclosure.'

'Yes,' Kara replied.

'Now, you see the fireplace is directly between the main hut and the calf enclosure.'

'Yes,' she said again.

'The path between the main hut, fireplace and calf enclosure is sacred. Until you have been made known to the ancestors, you cannot cross or walk on that path.'

'And the ancestors?'

'The fire is most sacred. It is always burning. That log burning smoke is the connection to ancestors.'

As they were speaking, headman Rutaka emerged from the hut. He walked to the fireplace and crouched down in front of it, fanned the smoke into a flame.

From where she sat, Kara could see the man's lips move in silent conversation.

Rutaka beckoned them forward.

The introduction was long and complex. Occasionally, Bird would translate a pertinent point or answer a specific question. Most importantly, Kara was now being accepted as a daughter of the village and a sister to Maveko.

When Rutaka was finished he added something else which Bird carefully interpreted.

'Rutaka's ancestors; his grandfather and his father want to tell you this. The men of the Himba desire modern things like radios and sunglasses, money and clothes. They think that this increases their authority. But the women do not want change; the women know that the old style of life is good, healthier, better for Himba community. The women fear the loss of their authority.'

Bird waited while the headman continued.

'Rutaka says that Maveko learns from you. You should instruct her that our old ways must be ….,' he struggled to find the correct word, '…re-affirmed.'

'You must teach Maveko that in the modern world of today, women have power. She must help our women to remember this and apply this.'

Kara sat there saying nothing, humbled by the dignity and wisdom in the headman's words.

'Maveko is clever, intelligent beyond her understanding. You must guide her, as carefully as we track when hunting.'

The fire seemed to flare up at these last words. Rutaka looked into it, his gaze lost in the crimson-yellow flames. The introduction was over.

★★★

From then on, Kara saw the Himba and their way of life in a different light. Their ceremonies were at times simple yet complex. Tasting the first milk in the morning required a small ceremony in front of the fire. Some clans were forbidden certain foods. Others were not allowed to eat wild meats and venison. Certain families were prohibited from owning livestock of a certain colour, this ban even extending to the colour of their dogs. Some groups could not even own dogs; others could.

The origins of many traditional rites were known to a few. Old men, who would pass on knowledge to their sons just before they died.

Central to all Himba activities is the sacred fire. Important rituals are always celebrated with a meat-feast and party.

★★★

Kara's interest in the women deepened. She observed their daily duties, watched how they moved ash from the overflowing hearths to a specially designated site near the calf enclosure. The large tortoise shells used as scoops were always kept in the same place.

Dung, like ash, was also always only collected by women. They made a dung stockpile for use when firewood was scarce. Over and over they built shelters and houses, as their men with the cattle followed the rain and grazing resources. Homesteads with permanent water were returned to at a time when all other reserves had been depleted.

The nomadic lifestyle was tough. Women bore the brunt of the work, collecting firewood, water, even caring for the livestock when the men drifted to far-off towns.

★★★

Childbirth was simple and natural, even when it was the first birth. Two or three women would attend the one in labour, who was not allowed to give birth inside a settlement's fences. Giving birth within a village would lead to mockery.

'You are giving birth within the kraal like a goat!'

Even when a woman was on her own, she would still leave the village for a shady bush some three or four hundred metres away.

Kara wanted it the same way.

Cathan was reluctant at first, but he did not need much convincing.

'The women will look after me. They were at our wedding; I would like them to be there when baby comes. And anyway you will be nearby too!'

When her contractions started coming regularly and steadily, Maveko and four others led her compassionately away to a clearing in some reed bushes. Spreading soft calf skins on the ground, the Himba settled her down with tenderness and care. And when little Matthew was born they sang as Kara cried in joyous relief.

★★★

They watched, seemingly unable to help.

After so many very dry years, the rains had come. There had been sporadic better falls the previous season, but now it was widespread. Gravel tracks turned into meandering rivulets, all the large flat areas were vast glimmering shallow lakes. The rivers were in full flood, carrying tree stumps, debris and drowned livestock down towards the Atlantic.

And in a u-bend, off the main stream of the Uniab River in a normally dry sandy gulch, Meme's adopted calf was struggling, powerless; stuck in a deep mud hole.

Cathan, Bird, and Kara who was holding fourteen-month-old Matthew, watched as the elephant group milled around the trapped animal in a clear state of anxiety and panic. Some of them were screaming and trumpeting, others were standing disconsolate, trunks hanging forlornly down.

Making matters steadily worse was the river itself. There must have been more recent rain in the area with the water level beginning to rise again. The young elephant was doomed to drown.

'We must do something,' Kara cried, 'Cathan, we must help them.'

'I don't think Meme will let us get near,' he said.

Cautiously he edged the Landrover closer to the elephant group. Meme flapped her great ears in a momentary sign of aggression, then turned away to face the stricken calf again. Her great feet ploughed the mud in frustration but she would go no nearer. Her intelligence knew the danger.

Bird and Cathan conferred quietly.

They drove away from the river, some two hundred metres up the bank, to safety.

Cathan spoke to Kara. 'Stay here with Matthew. Set up camp. Start pitching the tents. Bird and I are going to try something.'

'But I want to help, too!'

'I know, but looking after our son is just as important as trying to save that elephant.'

In minutes, they had unloaded. He kissed her quickly and then the two men were in the Landrover heading towards a large camelthorn tree. Looping a thick rope around a broad low branch, they tied the loose ends to the tow hitch on the rear bumper.

Engaging four wheel drive, Cathan tore the heavy branch down with a sickening splintered crack. Slowly they dragged it towards the river, to where the elephant was stranded. Only its trunk and the top half of its head were now visible. The remainder of the poor animal's body was submerged in thick, all-entrapping mud.

Bird loosened the rope holding the branch. Cathan swung the vehicle around, and they used the front winch to re-secure the branch. Then, playing out the winch, the two men slowly, back-breakingly slowly, rolled the branch into the mud.

Stripping down to his shorts and tying a rope around his waist, Cathan made his way in. Bird fixed the loose end to the Landrover as well.

Up on the bank Kara watched the scene unfold, all thoughts of establishing camp forgotten. It was unbelievable, almost surreal, suspense. Flooding water in the driest of places, troubled fretting elephants, her husband almost to his shoulders in mud and detritus, her son asleep through it all in her arms. Through binoculars, she saw Bird move carefully towards the elephant group. He seemed to be talking to them, his arms gently moving, his gestures placating.

'Are they are listening to him?' she thought, 'they seem to be calming a little.'

Cathan could feel the mud sucking at him, but his feet were still on the stony river bed. He knew that if the bed fell away any deeper, he would be in trouble.

Progress was painfully slow as he shoved the heavy log towards the desperate animal in front of him. The log too was slowly sinking, but the winch rope holding it remained taut, keeping a small measure of control.

He knew that there would probably be only one opportunity. If he could push the log to within range of the elephant's trunk there was a faint hope. The one thing he knew, and this it what he and Bird had discussed. If the poor beast could wrap its trunk around the log, there would be a slender chance, a once-off only chance, of trying to free it.

The young elephant watched with doomed, terror filled eyes as he struggled nearer. Cathan could feel the mud getting deeper. He could move no further. With a last strenuous push, the log was now just within the animal's reach.

He shouted to Bird.

'Pull me out. I'm sinking. Pull me out now!'

From the bank they stood and watched. There was an uncanny silence, a stillness, a waiting for something to happen. Or to end.

Bird pointed, '*luister*, listen.'

The air seemed to throb. There was a sound, a deep low shudder. A hushed pulsation, again and again and again.

'Meme is talking to her calf, I'm sure,' the little man whispered.

With a tentative movement, the elephant's trunk stretched out to the log. It lengthened, elongated further, now halfway over the log, then with a slight almost imperceptible heave the elephant grasped it.

'Let's try,' Cathan turned to Bird, 'now we have to do it!'

He engaged the winch and the steel cable tightened. But it would not rewind. Nearly two tons of large animal; a dead weight at the winch's limit.

'*Basie*, try and reverse the Landrover,' Bird shouted.

Thrusting the vehicle into four wheel drive, Cathan slowly tried to reverse. Still the weight was too much. He revved the engine a little more, the tyres bit into the rocky ground.

'Please God,' Kara breathed, hugging her son tightly.

The vehicle seemed to slip, to dig deeper, as Cathan applied power. There was a smell of burning rubber as the tyres spun. And then a slight jerk.

Backwards.

Cathan felt the movement. Carefully he accelerated again. There was another reverse movement.

Bird held up his hand.

'Look.'

There was no doubt. The elephant's head and ears were now above the mud, its trunk still tightly wrapped around the log.

Holding the vehicle stationary, Bird tried the winch again. It whined as it took the strain but there was a slight turn.

There was no doubt; if the animal could retain strength and continue to hold on, it would be saved.

Slowly, inexorably slowly, the winch drum turned. There was a sudden slackening in the cable. Only the log now being pulled back. They all watched as the calf hauled itself out of the mud-hole, stumbling as it reached firmer ground. With a high-pitched squeal it was free, lurching off towards the other elephants.

The group gathered around, their devotion affectionate. There were subdued muffled sounds of caring. Meme came close and the rescued calf leaned up against her.

The great matriarch looked straight across to the men as if there was something to be said. Minutes passed and still she stood.

Then the herd moved away up the far river bank and were soon out of sight.

Later, after Cathan had repeatedly washed himself down, Kara examined him carefully. The front of his body and his arms and legs were full of splinters and thorns from wrestling the log towards the elephant. These she removed, treating the areas with antiseptic. He had a broken finger as well, which she straightened and strapped to the adjacent middle one for support.

He sat quietly as she fussed over him. Then she was weeping, holding him, 'you were so brave, so strong, you saved Meme's calf. I love you so very much.'

Cathan held her. 'We all saved him,' he said faintly.

★★★

The next morning the elephant group was back, feeding and browsing near their campsite. The stress of the previous day seemed to be gone.

'I would have thought they'd have moved on immediately,' Kara stated, 'get away from here.'

'Mmm, I think the matriarch is re-establishing routine.'

Nightingale and her little calf were very close now. Nightingale's large eyes were calm and trusting, her posture inquisitive.

'Let's introduce Matthew,' he murmured, standing up unhurriedly.

Hesitant, Kara looked at him for a moment.

'Hold him out to her.'

Kara did as her husband said.

From about thirty metres the large female elephant observed them. Very deliberately she made her way nearer. Kara was shaking but Cathan held her arm firmly. He knew that friendship between man and animal is an amazing special thing. Nightingale's trust in them had to be repaid.

The couple were entranced as Nightingale stood just a few metres away. They watched as her great trunk raised out towards them. It swayed in leisurely half-circular movements above their baby and then with a feather-light touch on Kara's arm, it blew a warm sigh of approval across them. With a measured turn she re-joined her family group.

***

As he drove Cathan mused how quickly time passed.

Two years ago they had rescued the baby elephant. Two years ago Matthew was so little, just learning to walk. Kara, back at camp, now some three months pregnant. And Bird too, older, not as sprightly as he used to be.

Slowly they made their way back to the Swartbooisdrift base as long shadows from the palm trees stretched across the gravel track. There had been a report by the local headman at Ehomba of a black rhinoceros sighting. Searching for five hours, only its spoor was found; the animal had disappeared into an area of impenetrable thornveld.

Now it was time to return home. Three-year-old Matthew was sitting in Bird's arms on the back of the Landrover, singing a chanting bushman song that he had learnt from the old man.

'A splinter of stone which is white
A splinter of stone which is white
A splinter of stone which is white
Rrrru rrra,
Rrrru rrra,
Rru rra!
To scrape the springbok skin for the bed
To scrape the springbok skin for the bed
Rrrru rrra,
Rrrru rrra,
Rru rra!'

Cathan turned off the track and stopped to open the gate

leading up to his garage and workshop when Bird called to him worriedly.

'*Kaptein, daar is iets baie verkeerd*, something very wrong. Take Matthew, wait here.'

And he handed the little boy over to his father.

'Wait here,' he repeated, 'until I come back.'

Cathan had never seen Bird like this before. The man's face was fearfully stern, his voice harsh and rasping.

'Wait,' Bird said again, holding his hand up in admonition.

Then he was gone, rifle in hand, disappearing quickly around the nearest building.

'What has he seen?' Cathan thought to himself.

'Ssh, my son,' he said gently, putting his finger across Matthew's lips to quieten him. He looked around, trying to determine what was amiss.

It was then that the uncommon stillness struck him. It was always quiet here, but this was abnormal. Usually late in the day there would be smoke from the cooking chimney or the small generator would be pumping water from the river. Even the dog was not there to meet them. Sudden and frightening, a single rifle shot went off, the sharp sound blistering the quietness.

He shuddered as a cold brace seemed to wrap itself around his chest. Placing Matthew down carefully, Cathan reached into the Landrover cab, unclamping his rifle.

'You won't need it, my *kaptein*,' the voice so soft, breaking.

Cathan turned. The old coloured man was standing there, shoulders bowed, face looking down. His body was quaking as if some terrible ague had overtaken him.

'What is it, man?' Cathan demanded, 'what the hell is wrong?'

Bird could not answer. With a trembling hand he pointed to the far side of the house; then crouched down next to Matthew, with his arm lightly around the little white boy's shoulders. For a moment Cathan looked at Bird, trying to read the trouble from his old friend's face.

Turning away Cathan ran off, around the first corner and into the open yard central to the three buildings.

She was lying face down on the ground, half twisted, right arm extended in some despairing farewell.

Cathan fell down beside her. Reverently he turned Kara onto her back. He brushed the dust from the anguished, tortured face. She must have died in such agony and pain. Around where she lay, were the signs of her convulsions, scuff marks; she had been violently sick. Holding Kara tightly in his arms, he looked around; saw that she must have collapsed earlier and then tried to drag herself closer to the house as paralysis overtook. Before unconsciousness set in, she had managed to scratch something in the sand. Standing up and still holding Kara, he could just make it out,

CATH XXX

Cathan carried her to the terrace, where he lay her down carefully on an old straw mat. There were four bites; one high up on the neck, another two on her left arm, the last on her upper leg.

Slowly back tracking along the signs in the sand led him to the small outbuilding that was their bathroom. Through the open door he could see the snake, a three metre long twisted and half-coiled black-grey length with its head blown away by Bird's bullet.

***

'She didn't stand a chance,' he said hoarsely to Jan Steyn, his boss, over the radio telephone that evening.

'It must have felt trapped, attacked when she sat or bent down, the bites are all so high. I always warned her to be careful; look out for mice or birds or spiders.'

'Yes, my friend, a black mamba is so dangerous,' came the distant reply, solicitous and sorrowful, 'there is nothing one can do or say now. I will be with you tomorrow. We will dig her grave together, we will bury her together.'

'But Aunt Esme. And my parents?' Cathan hoarse.

'I will tell them,' Jan said.

***

On the far side of the Hartmanns Mountains, in a hidden valley down near the river are two hand crafted crosses. Above them, fixed to a large boulder is a brass plaque

KARA and LEIGH ANN

Place thy hand across my eyes so
that I may see only good
Breathe thy breath upon my lips so
that I may speak no wickedness
Whisper thy name in my ears so
that what I hear will soothe my soul
For when my soul is called by thee
it must come as clean and fresh
As the rain thou sendest
in the Spring of the year

(Herero Prayer to Karunga)

★★★

ATHLETE

I was sixteen, she was fourteen.

Siobhan had dark hair cut short, she was tall for her age, lean and strong, with the legs of an athlete and, in my eyes, the prettiest girl in the school. She could always run faster than me, in fact she could run faster than almost everyone except the senior boy runners.

Lewtin had asked her to be his girl, but she chose me. We were infatuated with one another, as teenagers are who for the first time fall in love. Little notes to each other, long telephone calls, whispered confidences, spending every available moment together.

A week after she'd agreed to be my girl, my grandfather died in England. When I phoned to tell her that we were flying out that night, there was no answer at her home. The school was on the way to the airport, so I pinned a letter for her on the noticeboard. Her family lived on the far side of the city. This was the only choice I had.

Dear Siobhan,

Thank you for being my girl. Thank you for being my first love.

My grandfather died yesterday and we are flying to England tonight. I've tried to contact you, but you must be down at the athletics track.

I just want to say that I love you and will miss you lots.

My mother says that we should be back in ten days time, after the funeral and when Grandad's estate has been sorted out.

I see our life together; I want to be at your side when you become a champion, I hope that one day we can marry and have children.

I have to go now, I will always be your boy
Forever, forever
Robert

When we returned some two weeks later, to my dismay she had left the school. Outside the boys changing room was a wire waste paper basket, empty, but for scraps of paper in my writing. I found my note, torn into four pieces. To this day I have it, carefully folded into my wallet.

I was devastated, it was if my life had come to an end. My studies suffered, I floundered in a daze; moped for hours in my bedroom.

I was just a young, immature boy, a boy who had lost his first love.

★★★

For the next ten years I followed her progress, in the newspapers, in the sports magazines and, as she improved, on television.

Her athletic prowess led to senior school

representation, then provincial; at twenty-one she had turned professional. The pundits said she was destined for Olympic glory, a Canadian sprinter who would win gold at both the 100 and 200 meter events. Siobhan was the quickest short distance sprinter of her era.

The pictures in the magazines showed that she had filled out; her litheness of youth was gone. I wondered how she had built the muscularity to her neck and shoulders; arms and thighs like a male body builder. And when I looked at her face there seemed to be a calculated hardness about it.

The year before the Olympic games, rumours began circulating of stimulants and performance enhancing drugs. At the World Championships where she had just won two gold medals, she tested positive. Both the A and B tests proved that Siobhan was guilty. The medals were taken away. An immediate two year ban was imposed. From heroine to total disgrace overnight; the Canadian public was furious at her cheating, it went against all their principles of fairness and honesty. The media went into a feeding frenzy.

Then the reports ended, I heard no more of her.

I always felt for her; there was still a love-ache that went back to my youth. The hurt of a lost first love stays with all of us.

***

My career was going well. I had initially started a Forestry diploma, but switched to become a doctor. At twenty-eight, after working at the same large city hospital for four years, I was now fully qualified. A five year contract with Management was agreed, after which I would go private and open my own practice.

I am glad that I made the change.

During my college years, I had become sidetracked. There was a time when I thought that a career in Forestry or Nature Conservation would be the right thing. But my parents, especially my mother, finally persuaded me. She always considered that the medical field was the right one for me.

In the adjoining hospice, whilst visiting a patient, I went into a room and there she lay. Her name was on the patient's notes in the nurses' station, otherwise I probably would not have recognised her. Reading the report revealed that she was totally bedridden, almost blind and deaf.

Moving closer to the bed, I speak, 'can you hear me, Siobhan?'

There is no response. Louder, 'Siobhan, can you hear me?'

At first she does not recognise my voice. Then slowly her memory starts to come back.

'Robert, is that you? Is that you?'

'Yes,' I answered.

Siobhan is quiet for a while. I stand there feeling numb, speechless, seeing her so wasted and ill.

Minutes pass. Falteringly she speaks, 'I said I would be your girl, but you left me.'

Trying to be gentle, I say, 'Siobhan, remember you left me, you left the school.'

'I was so distraught and unhappy, I did not know

what I had done wrong. The others said you had left for England. My parents felt it best to move me to another school.'

'But my note?'

'What note?'

'The note I left for you on the school notice board. Here it is, I'll read it to you.'

From my wallet I draw out the four scraps of paper, smooth them, place them together and read it to her.

Dear Siobhan,

Thank you for being my girl. Thank you for being my first love.

My grandfather died yesterday and we are flying to England tonight. I've tried to contact you, but you must be down at the athletics track.

I just want to say that I love you and will miss you lots.

My mother says that we should be back in ten days time, after the funeral and when Grandad's estate has been sorted ...

She is crying now, with whatever passion and limited energy she has left.

'I never saw it. I didn't tear it up.'

'Somebody else must have taken it then.'

She nods. 'It was probably Lewtin. He kept hounding me to go out with him, even after I changed schools. Why did you not try and contact me?'

To this I had no answer. Even if I did, how could I tell her of my past hurt and heartache, considering the present pain and suffering she was in. How could I accuse her. We were both so young at the time, she flighty, impressionable; me lovestruck, not thinking straight. Both sets of parents not understanding, or wanting to understand our feelings for each other.

'Rest a little, I'll come back in the afternoon and see you.'

★★★

My thoughts are in a whirl as I sit at my desk. Concurrent feelings of lost love, guilt and sympathy encompass me.

When I go back to her room later she is sitting up, propped by pillows under her head and shoulders. A nurse has obviously helped her put some make up on, the light dimmed to conceal the ravages of her illness. She is a bit stronger now, whether it is from rest or medication I do not know. We talk quietly, going back over the past years. My story is fairly short: finished school with high grades, university, working in this hospital, no wife or girlfriend, just the very occasional date.

She asks me what I do in my spare time.

'I enjoy hiking in the mountains whenever I can. And birdwatching. Very occasionally some river fishing but to be honest, find it rather boring.'

Her story is totally different. She tells me of the sport, the highs of winning, the lows of injury. The stimulants she knowingly took; to build her body, to train repetitively harder, to make her quicker and more explosive. The way her body changed; menstruation irregular then stopping, breasts muscled away, susceptible to every germ going around, catching colds all the time. When I question her about the stimulants, she tells me that is the only way she could compete against the East Europeans.

'The Russian, Caribbean and American women are also taking illegal substances. The authorities will have to accept this and allow athletes to decide for themselves. Or apply stricter controls. Until then, the problem will never go away. There will always be an athlete, trainer or manager who is prepared to cheat in order to win.'

We talk on about the corrupt trainers and managers, who seemed to suck away all the money she had made.

'I am not a good judge of character, I trust too easily. My focus was on running, winning; I tended to shut everything else out.'

But she is adamant about one thing. 'I did not knowingly take drugs before the World Championships, the winners are usually always tested. My trainer must have put them in my sports drinks, spiked my liquid intake.'

'Why, what motive would he have?' I ask.

'To get the cash, the prize money. We are paid immediately after the race, appearance fees are paid before. When the test results were announced, he just walked away from me.'

'Why didn't you appeal?'

'I tried. Nobody would help me, would listen to me. My parents are poor, I had to pay the prize money back. I had nothing left. I was an outcast.' She is crying now; weak, bitter sobs. 'I am an outcast.'

I take her emaciated hand and tell her to go on.

'About four months into my suspension, I started getting fainting spells, constant headaches, buzzing in my ears. I didn't want to eat, could not even keep food down, I was always nauseous. My parents gave me aspirin, codeine, vitamin C, anything they could afford, but still I became more and more ill.'

'And then?' I ask.

'They took me to the local doctor, who referred me here.'

'How long have you been here?'

'Six months. I have a brain tumour, it cannot be operated on.'

'What do the specialists say?'

'They say there is nothing that can be done. What caused it, who knows? The consensus is that it could well be due to the drugs I took in training, the side effects are unknown. Robert, they have told us,' she can barely say it... 'I...I have less than a month to live.'

I look at her; despite her suffering, I still see the fourteen-year-old beauty of my youth. The girl I loved.

Exhausted now, Siobhan sleeps a little. When she awakens I am still there. The night nurse comes in with Siobhan's medication and a glass of water. At first, not realising who I am, she tells me that visiting hours are long over. But when she sees my hospital badge, apologises, offering to bring me a cup of tea on her return.

Siobhan looks at me, her hand still in mine.

'My promise in the note still holds true. I will always be your boy.'

My voice is tremulous. 'If I could do anything within my means, anything to help you, what would you want me to do?'

She whispers, so softly I almost can't hear. 'To die as a wife, knowing that someone, you, will remember me; put flowers on my grave, will visit me.'

***

It took two days to arrange the wedding. My father went down to see her parents, explained the situation and brought them back with him. At her bedside that late afternoon were my family and her elderly mother and father. The two mothers, hers and mine, dressed Siobhan in a simple silk gown, long sleeved to cover her very thin arms. They placed my late grandmother's ring on her left hand.

With the consulting specialist, a gruff though good-hearted Scot, accompanying them in a firm baritone, the hospital choir, all nurses, sang Beethoven and Schiller's wonderful Ode to Joy.

Their voices rang around the room; down the passage where other people, staff and patients alike, were crowded.

Oh friends, not these tones!
Let us raise our voices in more
pleasing and more joyful sounds!

She gave us kisses and wine
And a friend loyal unto death;
She gave lust for life to the lowliest,
And the Cherub stands before God.

Can you sense the Creator, world?
Seek him above the starry canopy.
Above the stars He must dwell.

Her faith unable to quell her tears, the lady Methodist minister wept throughout the service.

Siobhan could only manage, 'I do, I do, I am so happy now.'

***

When everyone had left she was totally drained, almost comatose. She gave a small smile as I crept into bed with her, fully clothed in my wedding suit. Gently I held her frail desiccated body in my arms.

And in the darkness of the very early morning she was still and gone.

***

PHYSICIST

Batchev was easily the most intelligent person I have ever met.

A Bulgarian by birth, he became a world citizen as his genius and reputation preceded him.

He first came to my Vancouver practice complaining of a sore neck. There, during the next ten years, I would regularly treat him and then subsequently his family. Of the same age, we grew to become friends.

'Just call me Batch, everyone else does!'

Batchev was a small statured, dark swarthy man. When amused, his face would glow with goodwill to all around him. But his complexity could just as easily lead to a deep introspective solitude. His education had led to a PhD in Physics by the time he was twenty-five but in reality he was an intellectual inventor.

'Robert,' he would say to me, more than once over the years, 'intellectual property is the name of the game. You can sell great ideas properly structured to leading companies for good money and not so great ideas to arsehole venture capitalists for even more!'

At times he seemed to forget that not everyone was like him. Sometimes his frustration would boil over. His total memory recall, an ability to grasp complex ideas and theories quickly, and an inherent interest in all around, made him mentally quicker than everyone else. The video game industry was where he started. Founding a small company with two of his university friends, an idea was developed to improve memory and reality software. It took two years before he was in a position to approach the leading Japanese video game manufacturer. The company (i.e the idea) was sold. His story of the sale was incredible.

'I spent two months in Tokyo convincing their engineers that our software was sound. I had just returned to Canada when the Japanese confirmed that they wanted to purchase. Could we meet in London to sign the deal. What do you think happened?'

'I've no idea,' I replied.

'We're in these fancy offices in London, all walnut panelling and small chandeliers. The Japanese have an entourage of ten, there are two sets of lawyers, two secretaries and myself. What do you think happened?' he repeated laughing.

'Batch, just tell me the damn story.'

He laughed at my exasperation. 'The contract was ninety pages long; everyone was going through it word by word. Except me. I switched off; to be honest I was almost asleep. Eventually my lawyer nudges me and says that the last thing to do is finalise the price. I say thirty-five million. The Japanese say thirty-five million. The secretaries type it in.'

'And so?' I ask.

'Nobody mentioned the currency. Operating out of the United States and Canada I wanted thirty-five million

US dollars; the Japanese thought that, being in England, I meant thirty-five million pounds. That's what they paid, nearly double what I wanted!'

***

It was during this time that he fell in love. Julie was of Chinese origin, her parents arriving in Vancouver in the early 1960s.

Her parents, who had survived but not prospered, owned a small fast food take-away in Chinatown, an enterprise which somehow managed to sustain a family of six. Julie's three siblings were all boys. Batch once showed me the little restaurant; a humble double-storeyed building with an apartment on the upper floor and which, from appearances had, at most, two bedrooms. For years the family lived there and the children were raised.

This was how they met. Batch stopped in to pick up a take-away. Julie served him.

The girl he encountered was very pretty, but forgetful and disorganised. My first impression was that she was self-serving as well. Her high schooling had also been curtailed so that she could help her parents. Batch and Julie married while he was finalising his first big deal; a second project with another major corporation was being developed.

Their two children, a boy and a girl, were born in quick succession, barely twelve months apart.

In the early years of their marriage, I enjoyed visiting them. I found the mix of their marriage interesting. His intellect and worldly knowledge, her unsophisticated manner, somehow generated an air of harmony in their home. Their little children were handsome, dark like Batch but with Julie's beautiful facial features. They were like sleek little otters as they splashed in the swimming pool.

We would sit on the verandah whilst he told me stories of business and investments. His lawyer, an old varsity friend, had helped him double his wealth. High risk had paid well; low risk grew his base wealth steadily.

And then he would play his favourite music. The chosen artist was always Anna-Maria Ravnopolska.

He would explain the music to me.

'She is the world's greatest harpist and a Bulgarian like me!' he would enthrall.

'Listen to this Robert; she's playing a Paraguayan harp!'

It was stunning. The clear clipped bell-like chords drifting around us, the soloist's hand walking the bass notes within the rhythmic melodies.

Batch would sink in the music. Eyes closed, sometimes an uninhibited tear, his Slavic features creasing with the emotion that welled inside him.

'That is true genius,' he would whisper when the sounds ended.

After five years or so, I began to notice the changes. Not in Batchev, but in his wife.

His fortune and affluence had taken over.

***

The house they lived in was sold, a large estate purchased,

the double storey house renovated and expanded. Within two years her immediate family was living with them too. Julie's parents now occupied the adjoining coach house. The three brothers, two of them married with young children, lived on the upper floor.

Batch was supporting twenty individual family members; none of them worked or even looked for employment. Included were his own elderly mother and an alcoholic married sister, both still living in Bulgaria.

It was clear that his enormous wealth, by his own admission $US500 million and growing, was contaminating the Chinese side of his family. Their lifestyle became more and more lavish: fancy clothes, exotic cars and holidays at the most exclusive resorts in the world. They had all appeared to forget that it was his wealth that sustained them.

Batch's acquired family had become decadent, idle and wanton.

★★★

Batchev, in my eyes, remained relatively humble. He didn't seem to spend anything on himself. His work lifestyle was hectic; the marketing of his ideas took him away from home for long periods. But when in Vancouver, he maintained a low profile life, driving an old beat up Chev truck, frequenting the more down-market restaurants and shops.

Sometimes he would say to me, just a little wistfully, 'Robert, I wish it was just the four of us. As it was when the kids were born.'

But he had a strong sense of family duty. Her roots and his own humble background gave him the responsibility to care for more than Julie and his two children. I sensed that he felt duty-bound to provide for them all. But there were times when he said something, something off the cuff, that made me wonder.

But the one who changed the most was Julie.

She, in essence, became a professional shopper. Something had to be purchased every day. There were hundreds of pairs of shoes, clothes worn once and never again. Leather belts too many to be counted; fancy hats, expensive scarves. Batchev once showed me her boot cupboard, there must have been more than fifty pairs, many very similar. The children had far too many toys, some of which were still in boxes, unopened.

What struck me most, however, was how Julie lost her sense of fairness to the people around her. People who helped her; cared for her well-being and security when Batchev was away.

Amelia was a typical example. She was their housemaid and nanny, a motherly smiling Filipino, a regular diabetic patient of mine. It was as if she not only came to see me because of the diabetes, but also to gain a sympathetic ear from time to time. The first year she worked for them she received a cash bonus at Christmas, the second year a little less and thereafter nothing at all.

'Why, Doctor Robert, why does she do this?' she would say, 'I am honest and hardworking. That little extra money I could send to my family in Manila. It is not even equal to one pair of Madam's shoes.'

As absolute power corrupts absolutely, so Julie

changed. The vast wealth had transformed her completely.

No longer comfortable with them socially, I let our friendship run down. He remained a patient of mine for a while, but then that ended too.

★★★

Nearly ten years passed before I heard from them again. Well, really it was from Julie only.

Out of the blue she made an appointment to see me. I barely recognised her. It was not the beautiful, well-dressed woman I once knew, pampered by beauticians, couturiers; personal trainers and life coaches. Julie was almost a totally different person now. She was very overweight with bad splotchy skin. Her clothes were shabby, shoes flat and scuffed.

I tried to be careful; not appear to be surprised at what was clearly her changed circumstances, 'Julie, it's been a long time, how can I help you?'

It soon became apparent. Her health was not the motive for seeing me.

'Robert, I have tried everyone I know, but all doors remain closed,' her usually normal Canadian accent had become slightly pidgin Chinese, 'you maybe can help, maybe only person left who can help.'

The story unfolded.

Six years ago, she received a letter from Batchev's lawyer.

She showed it to me. It was brief and to the point. Batch would not be returning to Vancouver or to her. He would provide financially for the two children until they were thirteen and twelve respectively. At that time they would be offered the opportunity to live with him, in consultation with the social services and in accordance with the children's own wishes. All other financial support was ended immediately. The house had been sold; she and her entourage were on two months' notice.

The letter was harshly factual, so unlike Batch. I was astounded when I read it.

'What happened next?' I asked.

'We sold everything to find more money. Clothes, motor cars, furniture, everything. This kept us all going for nearly three years,' she replied, 'but then that money finished.'

'And the children?'

'As Batch wanted, they are now with him. Where, I know not. That is why I here.'

'You want me to find them?' I said, mildly incredulous.

'Batch is your patient; you must know where he is. You please ask him to help me.'

'Julie, I haven't seen or heard from him in a long, long time. I really can't help you.'

She looked at me, almost aggressive, not appearing to accept that what I had told her was true.

'Then you must help me with money. You friend.'

'I'm afraid I cannot,' I replied bluntly, irritated by her approach.

Julie lifted her finger to point at me, maybe to say something accusatory but stopped. With a resigned shrug of her shoulders she stood up to leave. A last curiosity went through my thoughts.

'Where do you live, what are you doing now?'

Her answer confirmed my suspicion. Her life had turned full circle.

'The take-away is re-opened, I live upstairs.'

★★★

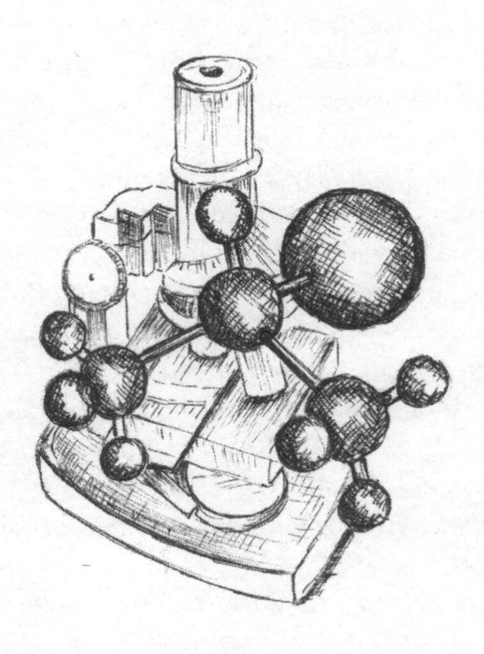

ROCK CLIMBER

On my way home from work one evening, I stopped at a favourite local restaurant for a quick meal.

The place was busy so the maitre d' gave me a spot at the bar. I was paging through a medical book whilst waiting to be served, when a cultured, very English voice said, 'that book was written by my uncle.'

To my right sat a good looking man, a year or two younger than I, with longish blonde hair and the tanned appearance of someone who does a lot of outdoor sport, a cyclist or cross-country skier type. But he seemed tired around the eyes, restless and unsettled.

We introduced ourselves. His hand was calloused and strong.

'My name is George Cameron,' he revealed.

'That's exactly the same as the author of this book,' I replied.

'Yes, it's an old tradition in our family, goes back many generations. My cousin bears my Dad's name, Alistair.'

When I questioned what he was doing in Vancouver, he told me that he was on his way to Stawamus Chief, planning to climb the rock face.

Stawamus Chief, known as the Chief, is the second

highest sheer piece of granite in the world. With vertical rock faces it is a haven for international climbers, who arrive with tents and in camper vans, setting off in the early mornings to climb the various routes. This explained his fit appearance.

When I asked why the Chief and why now, he looked away, sounded circumspect as he answered.

'It's the right time of the year, the weather's good. For us climbers it's also one of those you have to climb. Technically very difficult, but one that can be done in a day.'

My own experience of the Chief, other than scrambling the marked trails to the top, was of rock climbers running up and down these trails without shoes on and the distinct smell of marijuana wafting around the campsite.

'There's always a little dope when the boys are climbing. It either soothes the nerves beforehand or lowers the hype afterward. Some of them partake before and after!' he said, and we laughed.

It turned out that he was planning to hitchhike the fifty kilometres to the Chief, but as I had the next day free, offered him a lift. This would give me the opportunity of visiting an old friend of mine who ran an art and curio shop in the nearby town of Squamish.

We travelled up early the next morning. He seemed a little pre-occupied, contemplative, but not sullen. I dropped him off, he shook my hand, we wished each other well and that was that.

Or so I thought.

BRIEFLY

SQUAMISH BC

Experienced climber falls to his death

Experienced climber George Cameron from Oxford England fell to his death yesterday afternoon. He had just completed a standard route up the face of Stawamus Chief when observers on the ground reported seeing him fall. The RCMP are investigating the incident

I was astonished, more than astonished, dismayed. Reading the news briefs in the Vancouver Sun during my lunch break, there was the report.

Distressed by the article, I decided to contact the police and tell them of my encounter with the unfortunate man. The investigating officer, Inspector David Dobson came to see me the following day.

'Thank you for getting in touch with us. Please call me David. The information we have at the moment is sketchy. Anything you can tell us will be useful.'

'I can't tell you much, its just the timing and coincidence of it all.'

After he had finished taking my statement, we sat talking for a while. He seemed to be a decent friendly man with a calm, unintimidating manner.

'May I tell you something off the record,' he asked, 'something that must remain in this room?'

'Certainly,' I replied a little sharply.

He just nodded at my reaction to the inference of not maintaining confidentiality.

'The full report has not been given to the media. We are still trying to get to the heart of the matter, so to speak.' There must have been a quizzical look on my face. He went on, 'we believe that Cameron did not fall.'

'He was pushed?' I asked.

'No, no. We know that he climbed with a partner, a partner who, when they reached the summit, gathered up all their gear and then left, jogging down a hiking trail.'

'And George?'

'There is more,' the policeman said. 'Two ladies, hikers from Germany, have stated that George remained at the top, standing on the ledge that he had just climbed over.'

'And?'

'Apparently he stood there for a while, then just stepped off the ledge.'

'What? Are the women certain?' I queried.

'Ah yes, they were only about thirty yards away.'

This was beyond belief. There must been a very shocked look on my face.

Dobson looked at me. A sympathetic kindly look, as if he sensed that I was feeling troubled, even somewhat responsible. Could I have done anything? Should I have sensed that a tragedy was unfolding?

I was still intrigued. 'Why are you sure it was George Cameron?'

'That was the easiest bit. His passport was in a

money pouch beneath his shirt, he wanted be identified.'

'His partner, the one who climbed with him, has he come forward?'

An enigmatic smile ran across his lips. 'No, and I don't think we'll ever know who it was.'

***

The memory of George Cameron lingered with me, often distracting my thoughts and concentration. The incident niggled at the back of my mind, just would not go away. Was this one of life's mysteries, a chance occurrence that never rounds off with an explanation?

One afternoon a few days later the telephone rang. It was David Dobson.

He came straight to the point.

'Robert, I have George Cameron's parents with me. They would like to come and see you.'

'Do you know why?' I asked.

'Yes, and that is why I think you should see them,' adding astutely, 'may ease the uncertainty a little. I can also tell you that we have agreed to close our file.'

***

They were a refined couple in their sixties, Alistair a retired naval officer, tall and dignified and his wife, a gentle English rose. With a pot of tea on the table between us and my condolences out of the way, I asked them why they wanted to talk to me.

She was the first to speak.

'We want closure, to take George's ashes back to England. But we wanted to see you. About George. You were virtually...' her voice was shaky, tailing off as her emotions overtook her, 'you were virtually the last person to see him, admitting to seeing him and speaking to him ...'

'You see, we loved him so much. So very much. Our only ....' she could not finish. Her husband gently patted her hand as she openly wept.

Again, I repeated what I had told the police, adding that the whole incident was also playing on my mind. I somehow felt involved, felt culpable; a gnawing worry that I could have been able to help their son. My medical training should have detected something.

Alistair was quick to intervene.

'No, no, you need not feel like that. When you hear what we have to tell you, you will know more.'

George was their only child, with a passion for mountaineering. This passion was matched in time, when he met and married Laurence, a French lady, very pretty, and also an experienced rock climber.

The sad story went like this ...

There had been an accident in the Alps. The two of them were climbing a known route, George leading, when suddenly Laurence swung loose, smashing her right arm on a protruding rock. Something had gone wrong, a frayed rope, an insecure piton, a spring-loaded cam not cleaned or lubricated properly. Carelessness. Nobody really knew.

And then as she swung back, something snagged.

'What was it?' I asked.

Alistair exhaled sadly.

'Laurence had a knife on a lanyard around her neck. But it was not a releasable lanyard.'

'I'm not sure that I understand.'

'The rope and lanyard got caught up. Intertwined.'

Her inert flailing weight was slowly pulling George off the face. He tried to get down to her; then tried to pull her up to him. But every movement on the rope tightened the lanyard even more.

The man's face was disconsolate.

'The lanyard turned into a noose. More like a protracted garrotte.'

'Is there more?' I questioned as compassionately as possible.

Laurence frenziedly indicated for him to cut her free otherwise they both would die. But George refused. Realising that he wouldn't do it, she made the decision herself, managed to turn and unclip, and plummeted to her death.

'Our son was devastated. He had counselling, psychiatric treatment - everyone rallied around him. The rock climbing community was incredibly supportive. Climbers would pop in to see him, phone calls and messages from all round the world. Sometimes half a dozen of them would gather in our lounge. Usually after an expedition. They would laugh and swop stories, drink vast quantities of beer.'

'Gradually they helped him climb again, helped him overcome what he perceived to be his weakness and fear.'

'But why now? Why did he step off that ledge?' I

blurted out unthinkingly. 'I hope the police ...' leaving the rest unsaid.

'Oh yes, Officer Dobson told us what has been reported.'

'But why now then? Why if George had come through counselling did he decide to do this?' I asked.

It was his mother, through her tears, who answered.

'It was the first anniversary of the accident; to the day!'

***

The rock climbing community tend to look after their own. They close ranks. You must always do what is right for your partner, as Laurence had done to save George. And now as a friend had done for him. Sometimes one has to come to terms with assisted suicide - not question the right or wrong of it. Sometimes one just has to accept.

***

MINISTER'S WIFE

I found myself elected to the board of a local civic association.

We were all volunteers. The new chairman, a local entrepreneur, liked to hold the regular monthly meetings at his business office. There he could make use of his own staff and facilities to assist us in our duties.

In fact as soon as he took up the responsibility, his personal secretary was co-opted to our board to take the minutes, manage the paper flow, generally chase us all up.

Whether by design or coincidence, we always sat next to each other at these meetings. Even during the breaks we tended to remain in each other's company, drinking tea and talking quietly. In between meetings, there were telephone calls, mostly trivialities that could easily have waited until next we met.

And so the attraction grew.

Janine was a slender pretty woman, attractive in a way not easily noticed. There was something about her face which seemed to indicate Irish origin: hair dark russet, an expressive mouth and small finely-shaped nose. Normally downcast, her eyes, when they looked at you, were a pale ethereal blue. She wore no make-up, tended to dress conservatively, almost dowdily, and seemed to have little confidence in herself. Even her fingernails were cut short, unpainted; beautiful hands that she kept hidden.

It was during one of the phone calls that I asked her to consider meeting me, somewhere secluded, an out-of-the-way restaurant or bar.

But she shyly declined.

★★★

Unexpectedly, at the end of the next meeting, she slipped me a note I as was leaving.

Robert,

My husband is away on Thursday night and every third Thursday of the month attending church duties in Calgary. He only returns on Fridays. If you would like to see me, this is the address - 2618 Redwood Road, West Vancouver.

If you do come, please do so on foot and after nine o'clock when my children are asleep.

I really hope to see you but if you can't make it or don't want to, I will understand.

J.

A slightly different person to the one I was used to met me at the door. Her clothes were obviously new, a low-cut silk blouse hung loose over close-fitting slacks. She had make up on, eye shadow and pale red lip gloss. Her auburn hair, normally worn close to her head, in a bun or tight tail, now hung free, surprisingly long, down to below her shoulders.

A mature, becoming woman who, despite the warmth of the house, was shivering when I took her into my arms.

'I am a little scared,' she whispered, 'my husband must never find out.'

Janine led me to the couch. There we held each other and talked late into that first night.

'My husband Brian is a Calvinistic church minister, one of the more prominent religious people in Vancouver. He is very conservative and believes in the total sanctity of marriage. My father was an Anglican priest, I met my husband through him.'

'Aren't you risking too much seeing me?' I queried, 'a younger man, single, and all the ramifications this brings. I don't want you hurt or ashamed. In terms of your husband's faith, I am the devil personified.'

'It is a long time since anyone paid any serious attention to me. Has spoken to me the way you do. I know you are a decent man. Everyone sees me as the minister's wife, but you see me for myself.'

It struck me then. The courtesy and small compliments I had given her, sometimes inadvertently; it was an attentive craving she had been missing for a long time.

Her voice was softly resolute. 'I have thought about this a lot. I will deal with any situation that arises.'

During those first evenings I learnt more of her. Her husband insisting that she immerse herself in church activities: choirs, Bible readings, Sunday-school lessons, women's faith groups. A social life that to me seemed oppressive and suppressive.

Because I knew so little about her, I had to ask her why she married him. At first she would not tell me. But slowly she opened up.

'My father committed suicide. To this day nobody knows why. He left no note; my mother might know, but she never speaks of him.

When he died, I was only nineteen at the time, still young and immature. Brian was the one who helped us through it. He arranged the funeral, conducted the service. At the time I thought it was with kindness and sympathy, but knowing him now, I think it was for different reasons. He saw me as a suitable possession he could acquire. Someone to mould into his career. I was vulnerable and hurt, he offered a shoulder to cry into, arms to hold me.

You know, Robert, I remember so little of my father, strange as it may sound, but I am sure he would have objected to my marrying Brian.'

She carried on. 'Sixteen years of marriage to a man a lot older than myself. My life has gone past almost without substance. The only thing I have are my daughters. But now I have something more. You are here.'

★★★

Our love grew steadily during the coming months. In the beginning she would not make love. It was easy to understand why. Occasionally there were livid bruises on her upper arms and once, when she let me open her blouse to caress her, there was a blue-yellow contusion under her left breast. Not only was her husband difficult and obdurate, he was brutal as well.

'Janine, if he hurts you like this, I am going to have to do something about it.'

'No, Robert, you can't. It's a small price to pay. What he does is wrong, what we are doing is also wrong.'

'But why does he beat you?' I asked.

'I don't know,' she replied, 'it started after our second daughter was born. He is not very - what's the word? Virile or potent. Maybe hurting and forcing himself on me helps.'

'Janine, I love you. I am prepared to talk to him. I'm also a doctor after all.'

She would then smile, a loving consoling look, 'ssh my darling, Brian is in trouble, his dogma inhibits him, strangles his lust. He is a doomed man.....but he is a doting father and a good provider....' her voice trailed off.

And so for three years our clandestine relationship lasted.

***

One evening she brought out a blanket which she laid over the lounge carpet. Drawing me down beside her, she allowed me to remove all her clothes for the first time. Janine was one of those women, more beautiful naked than dressed. A wonderful unmarked body even after childbearing, legs firmly sculpted due to her passion for tap dancing as a child and teenager.

I was always very gentle with her, often using only

my fingers. When her orgasm overtook her she would shudder against my hand, crying my name softly.

But sometimes, however, her conscience would stifle arousal. Then she would lean over me, kiss me over and over, stroke me to climax, whispering, 'Robert, I love you, I do so love you.'

During the weeks when we did not see each other, I would ponder our relationship. We were both in our thirties. She was clearly in love with me. My love for her had a different base, a foundation that was built on a respect for her, her situation, a love that had grown steadily rather than rapidly. I missed not being with her, this gentle soft-hearted woman caught in such a difficult situation.

When we met in public, I maintained the same distance and courtesy as in the past. We were so careful that even Lorraine, a close friend's garrulous wife, did not notice.

Lorraine, who had known Janine for a long time, only once remarked, a little surprisingly I thought, possibly with a woman's intuition, 'you know Robert, its been a long time since I've seen Janine so happy and contented. I don't why, that husband of hers is a real bastard.'

Lorraine could be a little forthright.

***

In my own mind, I was ready to change our status. The furtiveness and secrecy was getting to me. Even though no-one knew of our situation, I just wanted it out in the open. I pressed Janine to decide; not forcefully or threateningly, just a persuasion that her life would be better. I would marry her or wait for her to be ready.

'I want us be honest with the outside world, with our friends, our business acquaintances,' I argued.

'My darling, you are very patient but I cannot leave Brian now. My daughters would be lost to me. He will never divorce me, it is too damaging for him in church circles. I would have to acknowledge infidelity. The courts will surely award the children to him. His career will also be affected.'

'But what about the abuse?' I questioned.

'It is only verbal now. I told him that if he ever hits me again, I would go to the police. Take the publicity that goes with it. That has stopped him.'

And somehow the knowledge that I wanted more from her would raise her sexual excitement, the guilt barriers dropping.

Janine knew that she was really desired for all that she was. 'Come on Robert, come on,' sitting astride me, moving herself up and down in long sure movements. I covered her mouth, kissed her as she became more and more vocal. 'Oh, oh my Robert, oh my darling,' she moaned into me, lying on top of me, quivering all over, as the ecstasy overwhelmed her.

***

'Robert, I need to see you,' her voice shaky on the phone. 'I can come to you, your house tonight. Please, my love, I will explain later.'

Her husband had been called to Toronto. In fact he had already left, it was a major promotion.

'Robert, do you know what he did?' she sobbed in my arms.

'What?' I asked apprehensively.

'Without telling me, he left taking our daughters with him. They flew out yesterday. While I was at work. I have already spoken to them. They are waiting for me there. I think he knew that I wouldn't follow if the girls were still with me.'

'I'll go with you, we'll confront him together,' I said.

But Janine was not convinced. 'He will not concede, I know it. The church will also protect him, especially after this move. The elders cannot be seen to have made a mistake in appointing him.'

The love we made was continuous, poignant, and sad; the only night we ever spent in a bed together. She cried a lot, but in the morning was composed. Later that day, I took her to the airport, embraced her tightly, told her to contact me at once if she ever needed help.

'My love for my daughters is as great as my love for you,' were her last words to me.

'You have no choice, they come first.'

Then she was away.

***

I only ever heard from her once again.

An unaddressed letter some four years later. It had been an empty, lonely time for me. I thought that I had got over her. But when Janine's letter arrived, I immediately tried to trace her; even employed a private detective to find her. But she and the two girls had left Canada, flown to London then straight on to Rome. There the trail ended.

In her letter she said that she truly loved me. She thought of and remembered me every day. It was my love and the memory of it that sustained her.

Her husband had committed suicide. He had been discovered molesting the son of one of his parishioners. Exactly the same offence her father had perpetrated, although he had never been found out, other than by her mother, who had, at last, told Janine the truth.

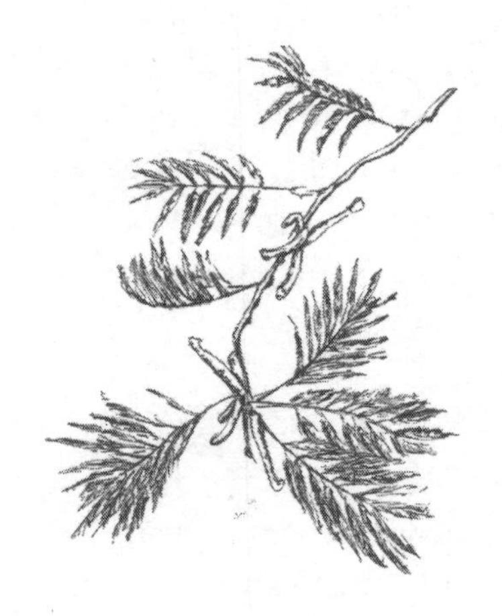

TEACHER

They shall grow not old, as we that are left grow old:
Age shall not weary them, nor the years condemn.
At the going down of the sun and in the morning
We will remember them.

These words, echoed by The Last Post, reverberated in my head as I made my way out of the church and walked down to the library.

Every year I attended the Remembrance Day service, but this year the ceremony seemed even more moving. What had made it special was not only the remembrance itself, the old soldiers upright in their uniforms, the poppies in the buttonholes and the elderly Womens Auxiliary members quietly drying their eyes, but the singing by the choir. Surprisingly, the men had ended their concert with Nkosi Sikelele Afrika (God Bless Africa), which for me carried a special significance. It reminded me of my friends who lived there, my contacts with Namibia, my affection for the bushveld and its wildlife.

The library was quiet that late Sunday morning. Not quiet in that there were no people; the place was busy but nobody was talking. Even the people checking their books out were whispering.

The situation became clearer as I approached the desk. The librarians were all wearing black arm bands. I had a sense that this was more than a Remembrance Day homage. When it was my turn I softly asked the middle-aged lady who served me, 'has something happened, Mrs Phelps?'

I knew her well. A personable, middle-aged woman, she regularly visited my practice with her son, a boy who suffered badly from asthma.

'Oh, it's so sad, Doctor,' she replied her voice catching, 'haven't you heard, Isaac died early this morning.'

***

The library in West Vancouver is, by library standards, a lively place. In addition to a vast array of books, a comprehensive music room is also incorporated into the complex. There are quiet areas, meeting rooms and, interestingly, teaching corners. These spaces are set aside for teachers to give extra lessons to pupils, all within the library environment.

Isaac Wolfsohn was one of these teachers. We first met at the little in-house coffee shop, when I asked him what he taught.

He must have been nearly eighty years old at the time. A very thin man, with a narrow face, grey bushy eyebrows and similarly grey hair, long down the back of his neck. But it was his eyes and voice that struck one.

They seemed so spirited, eyes bright and eager and a voice seemingly of a much younger man; firm, clear and resonant. I always thought that he drew this youthfulness directly from his pupils, the teenagers he taught mathematics, physics and biology.

I enjoyed chatting to him, an intelligent, wise man who had such a positive outlook on life. He lived for his pupils and their futures, his past he never spoke of. As with all good teachers his students adored him, there were always little gifts on his table and invitations to their scholastic awards.

***

The news of Isaac's death was distressing, considering the importance of the day. But I was to be even more touched two days later.

'We are holding a small memorial function for him on Wednesday, won't you come along? I am sure you would be most welcome. You were Isaac's friend as well,' it was Ann Phelps on the telephone, 'please do come!'

I found the home in the older part of Vancouver, an area settled in the main by immigrant Europeans, Germans, Poles and Russians. It was a sombre group that gathered that evening. I recognised the staff from the library and a few other people who seemed to be like myself, friends of Isaac.

There were three more, whom I did not know. A bulky bearded man in his forties and an elderly couple, the old lady confined to a wheelchair.

We had helped ourselves to tea and were talking softly amongst us, when the large man got to his feet.

'Thank you very much for coming,' he said solemnly, 'my name is Rabbi Nahum Rachmann. Our hosts are Moishe and Mary Levinson,' pointing to the old couple next to him.

'You may be wondering who we are,' he went on.

Rabbi Rachmann looked around the room.

'We are the connection to Isaac's past.'

The group was silent, expectant.

'Isaac and Moishe were the only two survivors of Dachau concentration camp still living in Vancouver; Moishe is now the last one. And I also have a link to Dachau. About two days before liberation, my father and thousands of other detainees were marched to the Ötztaler Alps. They were in a terrible condition, nearly all of them died, my father included.'

Ann, who sat next to me, spoke, 'why do you want to share these terrible things with us?'

After a pause, the rabbi answered, 'it has been Moishe's decision. When he and Mary married in 1952, they took Isaac into their own home, this house, where he lived until he died last Sunday. Never in all these years has Isaac spoken of Dachau or the past, either here at home, his work or at shul. It has been a large burden for this couple to bear; they feel that it is now time to shed it.'

'But why do you want to tell us about it?' Ann asked again.

'Because you were all he had. He worked at the library, lived in the back room of this house and went to synagogue very occasionally, sometimes only once a year.'

'He must have had friends, social activities?' I queried, 'what did he do on his days off?'

'Isaac had no friends nor wanted any. Holidays and time off were spent in his room.'

There was a lull, then everybody started talking at once.

Rabbi Rachmann held up his hand and smiled, 'why don't we all get another cup of tea or something stronger. Then we can continue.'

As everyone sorted themselves out, I sat back and reflected. I once went to Dachau. About ten years ago. There was a free afternoon at a medical conference in Munich and I had taken the opportunity to visit the concentration camp, now a museum and memorial.

I remembered it as a brooding and miserable place. Some of the buildings were well concealed. The first built crematorium is almost impossible to see from the camp and the ovens were in a wooden shed surrounded by trees.

However, it was the visiting school children that made the greatest impression on me. They arrived exuberant and noisy; after the photographs and film show they left in shocked silence.

'Moishe will show you where Isaac stayed; he will tell you more,' the Rabbi said.

Isaac's room was stark. The walls were painted white, a bed with a bare mattress stood in the centre, a small cupboard in one corner. There were no adornments, no pictures, no books, no curtains. It was like a stark prison cell.

'What have you done with his possessions?' one of the librarians asked.

'Nothing at all,' said the old man. 'These are his possessions, this is how he lived for over forty years.'

'I am not sure that we understand what you are saying,' Ann Phelps remarked.

'Isaac lost everything at Dachau; his family, his friends, his career, his dignity, his home and possessions. After that he was too scared to lose anything more.'

Everyone was disconcerted. I opened the small cupboard. In it were a few clothes, two pairs of shoes; a heavy jacket that he always wore on cold days. There was an old fashioned razor, a comb and toothbrush. Nothing more, nothing less.

'But what did he do when he was alone?' Ann enquired.

'Nothing,' replied Moishe. 'He would just lie on his bed, as it is, until it was time for him to go to work.'

He led us back to the lounge where the Rabbi was waiting. Once again, we all settled down.

The old man Moishe began speaking. In a slow, shaky accented voice, he told us the appalling story.

★★★

In 1938, Isaac and his family were incarcerated in Dachau. He saw his wife and their tiny daughter of two only once again, a fleeting glimpse in a group of women that were being marched off into the fields. His elderly parents did not last long in that dreadful environment, passing away about a year later, within six months of each other.

'Why was he imprisoned?' I asked.

'He was a Jew, a highly educated man,' came the reply.

'And what happened to his wife and child?'

Moishe shook his head, 'Isaac spent many years after the war trying to find them or a record of them. But without success. They were two of the many who disappeared without trace.'

A young librarian enquired, 'was he a professor or teacher?'

'No, no, he was a doctor. More than a doctor, a very skilled surgeon.'

The library staff looked at each other, surprise amongst them clearly evident. One of them was about to say something, when Moishe went on.

'Isaac tried to do his best for the inmates, but we were dying from disease and hunger. Typhus was rampant. He urged us to remove lice from our clothes and from one another's hair. But in those overcrowded, filthy conditions it was an impossible task. In 1939, Isaac's life changed for the better; and for the worse.'

'That is contradictory,' Ann Phelps exclaimed.

'Let me make it more clear. People were dying every day. Their bodies were taken straight to the ovens. The weaker or older prisoners were taken to the gas chambers first. Then to the ovens for incineration. Most of the stronger ones were marched to the arms and munition factories or other supply industries to work. But the strongest were doomed for the worst.'

'Why?' I asked, 'that is also contradictory!'

'They were kept aside for medical experimentation,' he replied.

'But how did this apply to Isaac?'

The elderly Jew looked at us grimly, his wife was trying to stifle her sobbing.

'In the early days at Dachau there were a least three Nazi doctors. As the war progressed, two were sent away to the Front. The man remaining behind forced Isaac and another prisoner to help him.'

'Help him in what way?'

'With the medical experiments,' he replied.

Our group sat there, numb and mute.

***

Moishe Levinson talked in a way that pierced one's psyche. It was simple, direct. I could see that some of the people present were becoming anxious, as if they knew that what they heard next would be gruesome and frightening.

It was Rabbi Rachmann who spoke though. 'I am sorry if this upsets you, please feel free to leave. We will not be offended.'

On edge, uneasy, we looked at each other.

***

Ann shuffled in her chair, 'go on, Moishe, tell us the rest,' she said.

'First I will explain what you consider to be the contradictions. When I said that Isaac's life became better, it did. He received a little more food, was allowed to shower, with soap and even had clean clothes once a week. It all sounds so little now. A small piece of meat instead of watery vegetable stew, an extra slice of bread.

But because of what he had to do, to be present at the experiments, it became worse. No person should ever carry the blame, the disgrace, that he felt and concealed for the remainder of his life.'

Some of the people in the room were clearly becoming more upset. Ann, who sat next to me, had her arms wrapped around herself. Consoling each other, two of the younger women were holding hands. An older librarian of about sixty had a handkerchief held to her eyes.

Moishe Levinson continued, 'the other contradiction is easily understood. The strongest were used in the experiments. They always died. Some of the weaker people survived Dachau and live to this day. Like me.'

'Are you going to tell us about the experiments?' I asked.

'All of you may understand Isaac better if I do,' he responded flatly, 'if you want me to stop, I will.'

Some of the experiments I remembered reading briefly about during my visit to Dachau, but nothing could compare to the first hand account that we heard next.

'I will tell you of two. There were more, some so horrific that Isaac never spoke of them,' Moishe said.

The first one he described involved simulation of flying at high altitude without an oxygen supply. A Jewish inmate would be placed into a chamber from which all the air would be steadily removed. At a simulated height of between 25,000 and 35,000 feet, the victim would die screaming and in excruciating pain.

Relating the second experiment, even the aged Moishe struggled to maintain his composure.

'The Nazis would make a prisoner wear a flying uniform complete with a helmet and life-jacket. He, or she, would then be placed in a bath of cold water. Water at a temperature of about 3° centigrade.'

'How long did it take for them to die?' someone whispered.

'It would vary,' Moishe replied. 'If the back of the head and brain stem was submerged, they were usually dead within an hour. If the head remained above the water line a few women survived, albeit unconscious and hypothermic. And then a further experiment was conducted. Even more hideous.'

'I can't bear to listen to this,' Ann stated, putting her hands over her ears.

'The Nazi doctor would then strip the unfortunate lady and rape her. The so-called test being "to bring her back to life." I hardly need to tell you that it never worked.'

Even my voice shook when I asked the next question. 'What was Isaac's role in all of this?'

'He was the surgeon. He had to observe, do the autopsies, write up the reports.'

Moishe Levinson looked around the room, spoke again, more gently this time.

'Be careful how you judge Isaac. He could not refuse, otherwise he would have been killed. Just another one of the thousands, no hundreds of thousands who were murdered at Dachau. He wanted to survive, just like me and many others; find his family again.'

There was a long silence.

Moishe went on, 'but every day the wind blew the smell of burning corpses across the camp, it generated total despair. A despair that one could not survive. That smell has never left me.'

He sighed deeply. 'Even on the happiest of days, when I married my beloved Mary, when our first child was born, that awful dread smell is with me.'

***

On a cold, rainy Saturday afternoon Isaac Wolfsohn was laid to rest. Fittingly, more than one hundred of his former pupils attended, all wearing red poppies attached to a small sign which read 'Always and Forever.' His acquired family was there to bury him.

The people that he lived for were there to say farewell.

But there was still more, something recondite.

As I walked to my car after the service, Ann Phelps called out to me.

'Wait for me Doctor, thank you for coming.'

Her eyes were red. She had been crying. I looked at her and the mystery lifted.

'About Isaac ...' she stopped me before I could say anything further, 'Isaac was the cleaner at the library for twenty-five years, a voluntary teacher for the next fifteen.'

'A janitor! And?' I asked.

'It was the Rabbi who saw the similarity. A week

after his death, Rabbi Rachman brought me proof, incontrovertible proof. Isaac was my father. You see, I also survived Dachau.'

★★★

FLEETING TOUCH

Keith

One evening during our holiday, my father and I were walking back from the central plaza in Trinidad, a small picturesque provincial town.

Picturesque in the sense of very old buildings decaying, and the not-so-old run down. And in between, people trying to repaint modest casas; the local authorities painfully and slowly renovating the more important and appealing structures. The smell of exotic plants in bloom; orchids and roses vying to overcome the odour of open drains and faeces, both human and animal. There appeared a sense of some external cleanliness, but it was superficial at best.

Saturday night in Cuba is party night. A ten-piece band played in the plaza. The music filled all the corners of the square. Electric piano, clarinets, congas and bass in harmony, deep trombones working with the drums. Two gorgeous and glittery lady singers, gyrating and swaying around a tall wiry man who sang in a high melodious tenor.

Couples of all ages were dancing: under arches, in doorways, out in the open, wherever the music could be heard and followed. The single men, mainly farmworkers and fishermen, were on the rum and on the prowl, lady tourists especially singled out for a vigorous and energetic salsa.

Robert

My dentist, who is also a close friend and, like myself, fond of the outdoors and travelling, married recently. It was a surprise to all who knew him. He had kept the courtship totally secret. We first met his fiancée at a small engagement party held only just a week before the wedding.

All his friends had thought that he was an established bachelor, teasing him consistently through the years. 'Women were just too smart for him, smart enough to avoid him,' and, 'just too difficult to tolerate.' And so on.

A big man, with a gentleness that belied his strength, Keith was about the most considerate and humane person you could find. He endured our comments with quiet good humour. The only child of elderly parents, he had looked after them and continued to do so even though his father was now nearly eighty-five, his mother having passed away some six years earlier. The home in which he had grown up was still where he lived, and where his wife-to-be was resolute they would remain when married.

***

Keith

At seventy-five, my father still thinks that he is a young man. His spirit and fitness amaze me.

'Keith, let's take a vacation, go somewhere interesting.'

'Where do you want go?'

'Cuba, let's go to Cuba. It's always fascinated me:

Fidel Castro, Bay of Pigs, Che Guevara, old towns, Hemingway, Havana - you name it, there seems plenty of interest,' was his suggestion for a holiday.

But he was tired now. Heading for the family casa where we were staying, we made our way down the cobbled steps. Approaching us, high-spirited and carefree, were three women, arm in arm. The lights down the stairs and from the houses shone on their faces. They were all very attractive, dark-haired and exotic. A middle-aged woman in her early forties and two younger ladies who were clearly her daughters.

As they passed us, the youngest of the three playfully stretched out her arm, gently running her hand down my side, softly pinched my waist.

Electric, erotic and quick; candidly sensual.

I grasped her hand, held it for a moment, stroked her inner arm from elbow to wrist. Something totally against my quiet, normally introverted nature.

She giggled lightly; I looked into a pair of the softest brown eyes, with a slight endearing crease between them.

Then we were apart in separate directions.

It was one of those destiny moments. I should have stopped, turned back, responded, but didn't.

A fleeting touch, gone in an instant.

★★★

Keith

On a glorious August day, I took the ferry across to Bowen Island and hiked up to the highest point. The views down the Sound were spectacular, across to West Vancouver, over to the far distant Lion's Gate Bridge. The beauty of the scenery rising to the immediate mountains behind. Sailboats played the broad channel; the first bald eagles could be sighted roosting, waiting for the autumnal salmon shoals.

Slowly I strolled back down the footpath, through the village, onto the jetty, waiting for the next ferry to arrive. Sitting in the sun, resting, eyes closed after the strenuous walk, I was momentarily startled when a voice next to me said, 'I wonder if you wouldn't mind taking a photograph of our group?' a lady asked, holding out a small digital camera.

'We are just at that table over there. It's our friend's last day in Vancouver and we would all like a memento.'

I looked across. There were about eight women gathered around someone in a wheelchair who was turned with her back to me.

'Sure, just show me which button to push.'

***

Conchita

'One Saturday afternoon my mother and I took a taxi to Cienfuegos, it's about eighty kilometres from where we live in Trinidad. My uncle had invited us to the cock fighting. It's very macho. The man who has the strongest bird can make a lot of money, earn much respect. My uncle's prize cockerel was big; confident and aggressive, with a high head and powerful neck.'

'But that's so cruel. It's as crude as bullfighting. Animals provoked, killed to satisfy some perverse form of bloodlust'.

She deflected the sharp, almost insulting statement with graceful ease.

'No, we don't see it as cruel. It's a way of life, ingrained in the poorer people's traditions. The government doesn't like fighting. They say it makes even more people poor, to lose money on betting. Try to ban it. So the fights are held secretly. But sometimes I see the police chief there too....'

With a knowing smile she hesitated, then continued.

'Our taxi driver saw the oncoming car and slowed down as a sharp bend was ahead. But the approaching one just kept its speed, missed the curve, then all went black.

Despite Cuban medical care, which is very good - the staff are well trained - I lost the use of my legs. There was nothing that could be done. I have not walked since that day.

Also from that day, my uncle gave away all his birds, stopped gambling. He felt so bad. His hobby, no, his passion, that also made him money; he believed that this was the cause of my disability. Every week on Friday nights when he drinks, he cries for me.'

The memory of it all, for a moment, brought a perceived change in her beautiful face.

'But what about the other car and your mother?' one of partygoers asked.

'Luckily, no one else was hurt. Just a few bruises,' she replied, 'the other car was rented by a Canadian couple,

Carla and Alan Webber. Carla was driving that day.'

'Carla is the lady that asked me to take a photograph,' Keith told the group.

'Yes. I think she has suffered more than me. I know that I will never walk again, there is nothing that can be done.'

Carla Webber was a woman driven by remorse. For years she tackled the officials, trying to obtain permission for Conchita to travel to Canada for further examination.

The Cubans were difficult beyond belief. A concession to an exceptional circumstance was seen as a sign of weakness, of favouritism to an individual, against the social welfare of many. In a country where it is virtually impossible for an everyday citizen to own a motorcar or even a cellphone. Where one is not allowed to use the internet. Where the state controls all. Anything that could be construed as tolerance, as sympathetic, which could encourage an individual's right, was almost impossible to overcome.

Impacting directly on Cuba was the collapse of its benefactor, the USSR. To offset this the Cuban government was forced to open up tourism, with Canadians steadily being the most numerous visitors, and the numbers were growing. Carla lobbied this as a lever to persuade the authorities to change their minds.

Eventually, after nearly ten years, Conchita had been granted a passport. It was to no avail. The treatment given to her by the Cuban doctors was as good as their counterparts in Canada.

'During this time, because of Carla, her coming to visit me every year, because she was always writing, staying in contact, I learnt to speak English, even reply to her letters. My grammar is not so good, but we all laugh and understand!'

Her voice was an excitable vibrant mix. Despite being trapped in a wheelchair, she was by far the most exotic and intriguing woman in the room; withered legs concealed by vivid pink shiny slacks, a silver-sequined clinging blouse, chains and jewellery. She glowed with life, the Canadian women around her were like dull moths attracted to a vivid candle flame.

'Because friendship is so important to us Cubans, a link that binds us, we have a Marti quotation which goes,'

'Who is Marti?' Robert interrupted.

'He was one of our liberators. One of our great men. A fighter and a clever man, what do you call it, yes, an intellectual. This is what he said,'

They say that one should take
The finest jewel from a jeweller,
I take a sincere friend
And set love to one side.

And although I cannot walk, I am very lucky. I have a sincere friend in Carla and now that I have found Keith, no longer have to put love aside.'

★★★

Keith

They positioned themselves for the picture and I took one. But looking at it in the camera's viewing screen, I could see that the group was too far away, too tightly focussed and not clear enough.

I stepped nearer. Centring the focus on the face of the lady in the wheelchair, I took another shot.

I looked up astounded, as if hit by a bullet.

The soft brown eyes, the little endearing crease; it was a face he'd never thought he'd see again.

Of a woman with a fleeting touch.

★★★

PART 3

Hours passed, I was thirsty but not tired. The names of the people I knew continuing to resound in my head.

Uncle Jim and Aunt Marge still living in Africa, I had last seen them about five years ago. She must have loved my father. And Uncle Cathan who had never married again. Now I knew why. Poor beautiful Kara.

Pamela, who had comforted Mom so much these last two weeks. What she must have gone through when her husband Chris failed to return from his second trip to Darfur. I knew about this, but not the detail of the first expedition. Their Sudanese children now so involved in relief work.

My mother was asleep in her chair as I walked to the kitchen, stick across her lap. Rhys, the labrador lying on the floor next to her thumped his tail twice in greeting as I passed. I bent down and patted him, moved on to make coffee.

Turning the battered cover, I opened the last part of the manuscript…

EXPIATION

James Mills, an English friend, is a man who has been solitary and unfortunate in love, his misfortune being with the women he meets and falls in love with.

He had been married for less than a year when his wife Jessica died whilst visiting the USA. An old schoolfriend of hers was getting married in Washington, the hen party was due the next day. Answering a polite knock at the door to their small home in Oxford one evening, the two attending policemen were solemnly compassionate as they gave James the news.

'She was killed crossing the road,' the older official said.

'What...ha..happened,' my poor friend stammered.

'She was out jogging, probably forgot for a moment that the traffic flows in the opposite direction, looked the wrong way. The driver of the car that hit her said it all happened so quickly. He couldn't stop. Our colleagues in America say that he cannot be blamed.'

***

Out of this adversity came instant wealth. James inherited a four million pound family endowment and was immediately financially independent.

Jessica had been an only child. Her father, Michael

Hardcastle, a retired executive, a shrewd and kind man, helped James through that difficult time. His own wife had also passed away, a cancer victim some five years earlier. This drew them together into a bond as close as that of father and son.

The older man was beneficent and generous. When James took over the care of his eldest sister's daughter, Michael became a doting, all-caring foster grandfather.

The two men nurtured and often fretted over Caroline, whose own circumstances were equally tragic. James's sister had married a South African business man and lived in Johannesburg. One evening as he pulled into the gateway at their home he was shot in his motorcar, through the glass of the side window. An absurd irony, as no normal citizen drives through Johannesburg these days with open windows or unlocked doors.

The black men slashed the seatbelt, pulled her father from the car, flung him into the driveway and made off with the BMW.

Eight-year-old Caroline, waiting for him to come home, watched him perish, contorted on the gravel. She could clearly see the terrible wound, her father's face awash with blood and yellow cranial gore. From the lounge window the murderous faces were unhurriedly visible. It was what she remembered most in later psychotherapy: the evil casualness of the incident, there was no rush or shouting. The assailants took their time in getting in the car and sedately drove off in order not to attract unwarranted attention.

Of their faces, she remembered nothing, had no recall. A lapsed total rejection.

After the funeral, his sister asked James for help.

'I have to get Caroline away from here, she spends hours looking out of that window staring at the spot were her father died...' she could hardly complete the sentence.

'Her brothers are bearing up better, they are still so little, cannot really comprehend what has happened.'

'But what about you?' James asked, 'why don't you all come to England, I'll look after you.'

'No, my life is here. I am going to take over the business. There are so many people dependent on it. Try and sell this house, find a new place to live but still stay in South Africa. It's not easy to sell a blood home here.'

She paused. 'If Caroline will go with you, I know you'll care for her. She can come back in her holidays.'

So Caroline lived with James. Every day he took her to school, she had counselling, made friends; steadily buried the pain of her father's violent end. Holidays were always spent in South Africa. Normally Michael went with her, both for his own enjoyment and out of his grandpaternal love for her. She had become the grandchild he always wanted.

***

James's life settled into a steady routine. The solitude after his wife's death diminished. He resumed his architectural work, but now on a freelance basis. His wealth grew steadily due to Michael's wise advice. A larger home was purchased and an office created on the ground floor. Work was taken on flexibly, most of his spare time spent caring for Caroline.

There was an odd casual date, but somehow the memory of what he had lost, Jessica's death, suppressed any active longing for further romantic relationships.

★★★

'Oh, damn it,' she scratched through her handbag, 'I must have left my mobile at home.'

Her car had jerked to a standstill. Opening the bonnet proved to be useless as she had no idea of what was wrong or where to look.

The local country road was quiet that warm afternoon, the time between the school run and people returning from work. After about fifteen minutes she heard a vehicle approaching. Tentatively she half lifted a hand, having never done this before, trying to hitch hike or flagging someone down.

The driver drew up just ahead of her. As the car switched off, she felt anxious, slightly scared. Its engine ticking in the heat was the only sound. A momentary flash of danger went through her mind. 'Too many late night movies alone,' she thought.

A good looking fair-haired man of about forty approached.

'Thank you for stopping,' she said, 'my car has broken down.'

'Let's put your warning lights on and I'll take a look,' he replied quietly.

She watched him as he bent over the engine. He looked fit, in good shape, as if he worked out regularly; his back muscles well defined in the light shirt he was wearing. His hands she specifically noticed; slender, with long fine fingers.

He looked up at her and smiled, blue eyes centred above a rather angular nose.

'I think it's just a loose battery connection. Try starting it now.' And it was just that.

'I'll follow you to the main road; see if the lead really was the problem.'

At the junction she stopped again and got out to speak to him, touching his arm lightly. A subtle, inescapable contact.

'Please let me have your name and address, I must write and thank you, I don't know what I would've done otherwise. My name is Elizabeth.'

'It's really not necessary,' James said. Nevertheless he gave her one of his business cards.

★★★

During the course of the next two years they grew steadily closer. Her thank you note led to a lunch date, to occasional evenings out; then they started seeing each other regularly.

James was slow, reticent; Elizabeth the more forthcoming. She was a tall, handsome blonde woman, with a full figure shaped by regular aerobics and Pilates classes.

Their backgrounds however, were quite dissimilar.

'I grew up in rather humble surroundings,' she told him soon after they met, 'my father was the groundsman at a private school. We lived on the school property, never really had a home of our own. My younger brother works there now, just like Dad. But I've been fortunate, did well at college, managed to get financial assistance to do a degree.' She was now employed as an accountant for a large computer company.

James only found out about his origins when he was fourteen.

'My father earned a good living. His affluence meant that we all went to good schools, all three of us graduated. I went to Oxford, my sisters to different colleges at Cambridge. They are both highly qualified. It was only when I was in my teens that my parents told me that Mum was in fact my step-mum. Made no difference to me. I grew up in a loving, comfortable environment.'

'Did you never try and find your true mother?' Elizabeth queried one evening, 'or find out what happened? Surely you must want to know?'

'No, I had no need to. I adore my Mum, she has been truly wonderful to all of us. Treated us all the same. I was told there had been an accident at childbirth. Without being told, I assumed, no accepted, that she had died having me.'

★★★

They were now deeply in love. Elizabeth wanted to go further. She tried to initiate James into making love to her, to start living together, but James was adamant.

'We have to pass the Caroline and Michael test first,' he insisted, 'everyone must be happy and settled with our relationship.'

He need not have worried. Both the old man and

Caroline, now a precocious thirteen-year-old, knew that James had something missing in his life. He deserved the love of a woman.

Elizabeth's relationship with Caroline was that of an older sister. Elizabeth helped Caroline through the nuisance of first menstruation and personal health, far better than James ever could. They did things together, visiting stores and shops; giggled over celebrities' antics in the tabloid magazines. It was not contrived or condescending; they just got on well together.

Michael watched the situation with calm contentment. He observed Elizabeth closely and liked what he saw and heard. She had filled a vacuum in all their lives.

Sometimes a movement of hers, or a gesture, would puzzle him; not unpleasantly, but in an ephemeral flicker, it was gone.

***

'Michael, I want to marry her, need your blessing,' was James's cautious approach, now more than two years after he and Elizabeth had met.

'You don't have to ask me,' came the response.

'I have to. It's because of the inheritance. The money I have now came from you and Jessica.'

'No, the money is yours. What happened to Jessica so long ago was a tragedy, but life turns and moves on. You both have my support.'

That night in James's bedroom they made love for the first time. With just a bedroom table light burning, their well-matched bodies turned and shadowed in shapes on the walls. When they were spent Elizabeth was crying, her love for him turning to tears. Softly he kissed her face and eyes until she was calm. And then they slept.

★★★

Two weeks later came the telephone call.

'I'm coming down to see you, old boy. We must meet, its very urgent!'

Michael's normal slow, well dictioned voice sounded anxious and strained over the line.

'Of course, whatever is the matter?'

There was just, 'I'll see you in a few hours.'

James sat wondering what the problem could be. Had something happened to Michael? An investment gone sour, or was he ill? A cancer threat? Or something to do with Caroline, although this seemed unlikely. She was due to be collected from school later that day.

When Michael arrived, he was clearly agitated. His usually genteel and controlled manner absent.

'I've checked into Elizabeth's background. I don't know why, just had a sense.'

'Sensed what, this seems very underhand, not like you at all,' James exclaimed, surprised by his own antagonistic tone.

The old man's face was tired, worn with worry, 'I know and I do apologise. But it's not underhand, it's so above board, so obvious, the more you look.'

'What is? Look where?'

'James, come with me to the mirror in the hall, look into it.'

'Whatever do you mean?'

He led his friend, his son-in-law, and the guardian of his precious beloved Caroline over to it.

'Now close your eyes and imagine Elizabeth's face.'

'What? Why?'

'Please James, look. Look carefully, close your eyes, think of Elizabeth!'

James stood there silent, concentratingly still, his face turning slowly grey.

'Oh, my god. I don't believe this.'

'Yes, but I'm afraid it's true.'

With slumped shoulders Michael said softly, 'I don't know what we are going to do. The mother you've never known and yearned for, is Elizabeth's mother too.'

***

It had been four years since we had last touched each other. Holding hands, standing at his still open grave, looking down at the casket, the sadness of Michael's death was all but nullified by the joy of being with Elizabeth again.

My mind went back to the meeting a few days earlier, where a pedantic old-world solicitor in a dull London legal office handed over a letter to me.

The letter was with me now, in the inside pocket of my black jacket. Why I do not know, maybe to remind me to say a silent thank you as I throw a handful of soil onto the coffin.

'Mr Hardcastle's instruction was for me to give this letter to you personally as soon after his death as practically possible.'

The solicitor's precise voice continued. 'He further instructed that you should read the letter in my office, consider its contents carefully and instruct me further should you so desire. The cost for my services if necessary would be borne by his estate.'

Michael's flowing handwriting, though now aged and shaky, was unmistakable.

My dear James,

The respect and love you have given me all these years shames me. Shames me in what I have put Elizabeth and you through. I can never know how much happiness you both have sacrificed in respecting my wishes by not getting married, once I found out the truth about your mother.

I must also tell you that Elizabeth has suffered greatly. She came to see me some six weeks after I dropped the bombshell with news that she was pregnant with your child. Together the two of us arranged for an abortion to be done by a specialist friend of mine.

I know that she has never told you of this. And please don't blame her.

I am so ashamed.

One can never atone for a word wrongly uttered or a deed done that, in hindsight, and with greater thought, need not have been done.

But luckily I still have time to write this letter. The same specialist that operated on Elizabeth says that it is unlikely that I will last another month.

Go to Elizabeth now, she still loves you very much. She always asks after you and tells me how much she misses you. I speak to or see her every week. The secret remains with the three of us.

Mr Howard-Price, my solicitor has been instructed to help you with any arrangements that need to be done and to ensure that the money I have left the two of you, should you exercise my original marriage blessing given four years ago, is carefully and securely invested.

James, should you choose to remain single, a situation that I would completely understand, Mr Howard-Price will ask you to sign an instruction that will give Elizabeth the full amount.

Elizabeth is a forgiving lovely woman. Your happiness is my last, most important wish.

You have my blessing. I should never have taken it back.

Yours,

Michael

★★★

PIANO TUNER

I was on my annual Namibian visit to Marge and Jim's farm when I met her.

Marge was preparing lunch when I arrived.

'Oh, Robert, it's wonderful to see you,' Marge said, drying her hands and giving me a brief hug, 'come and meet a guest of ours.'

'Helena, this is our great friend Robert, doctor, birdwatcher, fitness fanatic, and all round good guy.' Her American exuberance never to be stifled or changed by Africa.

'Robert, this is Helena de Villiers, she is staying with us for a few days.'

She was sitting in the shade of an umbrella by the swimming pool; a golden Labrador lay alongside to her right, close to her. It was then that I noticed the dog's luminescent harness; a white stick stood propped up against the table.

Her right hand extended in the direction of Marge's voice and I shook it lightly.

'I'm pleased to meet you, Helena.'

'And I too am pleased to meet you, Marge has often mentioned your name.' Her voice was very restrained, slow spoken, almost as if she was not accustomed to talking.

'Good, I will leave the two of you to chat while I finish preparing our lunch.'

Marge disappeared back into the kitchen.

'My dog's name is Rusty, if you come around here, he will greet you. He doesn't leave my side.'

After lunch I continued to sit with her. She was about twenty years younger than I, in her late twenties, maybe just thirty. Most of her face was hidden beneath a sunhat and an old-fashioned large pair of dark glasses. Her clothes too, slacks and a simple blouse, also looked slightly out of place, outdated and, although clean, rather shabby. She and her mother lived in the nearest town, about fifty kilometres away. Her mother was the nurse at the clinic; Helena gave a few piano lessons and did piano tuning.

It was Marge who told me the next day that Helena was very poor, that there were not that many pianos to tune and the lessons she gave were mainly to black students, students who could not afford to pay but who sometimes brought vegetables or some fruit in gratitude.

★★★

Later that same afternoon, the first day we met, Helena surprised me.

'Would you walk with me in the veld?' she asked, 'I have never done it before. You must also tell me what you see ...... birds, animals, and please describe them as well.'

We walked along a track down to the river, I led the way just in front of her. Leaving her stick behind at the farmhouse, her right hand held Rusty on his lead. She placed her left hand on my shoulder to be guided. Something inside me shook. Just her contact was enough.

In the open air and late direct sunlight, I could see that she was stunningly beautiful. High cheek bones and a full, expressive mouth, her skin completely unblemished. A small breeze blew through the thorn trees. Her hair, a dark gleaming brown, lifted off her shoulders.

'Robert, tell what you see. And what is that shrill, buzzing sound all around us?' she asked.

'Those are cicada. Large insects about three centimetres long. Once one starts up, all the others in the area get going.'

'How do they make the sound?'

'It is interesting,' I replied, 'they have thicker membraned ribs which are called timbals. When the cicada are alarmed or excited, they vibrate these timbals, rapidly, which cause them to click. Their abdomens act as amplifiers. That is what you hear.'

At the river we crossed over the sand bed to the other side and made our way up to the dam. As we strolled together I told her of the birds, little wood hoopoes with their tufted heads alert, a lilac breasted roller. In a large tree some distance to our right, a brown snake eagle stood on the top branch. There were warthog drinking at the cattle trough, darting off, tails vertical, when they saw us coming.

I did most of the talking, she content to listen as I rambled. It was all new to her, enchanting and enthralling.

That night when I went to bed, it was a struggle to sleep. Helena's low voice kept circulating in my head, envisioned by her glorious face. An awareness was growing. I wondered, hoped, that it was mutual. I could not tell if my attraction to her was based on sympathy, empathy, protectiveness or something deeper.

At dawn the following morning, when everyone else was still asleep, I went for my usual long run along the farm roads. Returning to the farmhouse, I plunged into the pool to cool off. There was a bark and a splash. Rusty, typical retriever had joined me, trying to grab me by the arm and pull me to the side. I lifted him out, climbed out myself when I heard her calling for him. It was a worried and slightly frantic plea.

'Rusty is with me. He has been swimming. We are coming to join you.'

I explained to her what had happened and she gave a small smile.

'Yes, he is a wonderful guide dog, but can be a little naughty at times. Sometimes at home he will run off for an hour or two. Walking along the roads, but still waiting and sitting at the road crossings and stop streets. When my friends bring him back they say that is very funny to watch, as if he is exploring with an invisible person at his side. He's also very pleased with himself, innocent, not guilty at all!'

The next few days settled in a leisurely routine. I would run in the mornings, have a dip with Rusty, read, then spend the afternoons with Helena.

Her life was very simple. She had been born blind, to a single mother whose husband had departed the day she gave birth to a daughter and not a son. In the beginning her mother had planned to move back to South Africa, but this never happened. They had lived in the same town, in the same house, for twenty-seven years.

'I have never travelled, never left the village. My mother looks after me, buys my few things,' she said simply. No remorse, just a little wistful.

'I learnt to read Braille and play the piano. Like many blind people, my hearing and sound co-ordination is very good.

Rusty is my first guide dog, I've only had him two years. It has made me more independent. I can walk to the shops on my own now.'

I knew that I was falling in love with this quiet, obviously intelligent, damaged, beautiful woman. Each morning when I saw her, my heart would go out to her. I wanted to hold her, take her sunglasses off, look into those non-seeing eyes and tell her what I felt.

'You look a bit moonstruck, old boy,' Jim remarked one evening whilst we were having a beer together. 'Marge says that Helena is also in some turmoil, her woman's instinct tells her so.' This was also said with a small smile.

I just nodded but could not speak.

***

We sat on the bank of the dry riverbed in the shade of a sweet thorn acacia. The small birds were chirping, turtle doves calling, their sounds endearing in the late afternoon.

'Helena, can I hold your hand? I want to tell you a story; a true story, a story that takes me back nearly thirty years to when I was sixteen.'

Looking my way, her hand stretched out to me. 'I've never held hands with a man before,' she whispered.

In that clear African air, with nature, the bushveld around us, I told her about Siobhan, the whole story, leaving nothing out, and that I had been married; for less than one day.

She wept through the last part, but did not let go. At the end, after I had given her the old torn faded letter to feel, I asked gently, 'Helena, will you be my girl?'

She went still. Slowly her right hand let go of Rusty's halter, moved up to my face, wiped my own tears away, traced the outline of my forehead, around my jaw, briefly touched my lips.

'Please take me back to the farmhouse,' her voice so subdued I could almost not hear it, 'please, Robert, lead me back.'

However, this time when we walked she did not rest her hand on my shoulder as she normally would, but continued to hold mine all the way back.

Leaving me, she went straight to her room and did not emerge until the following morning.

Jim, Marge and I sat that evening around the fireplace. I told them that I may have upset Helena and if so, would leave the following day. It was not fair on anyone for there to be unhappiness. Neither of them said anything. A look passed, unspoken words.

After a few quiet moments I excused myself and went to bed, to lie there sleepless till the darkness eased and I could set off on my early morning ritual of a run and swim.

When I got back from my run, she was waiting for me. I, uncertain, hesitant, almost dreading what she might say. All I had thought of during the previous night was whether, at long last, Helena would be the woman for me? Would this all work out? Certain in my love for her, could she change her life to be with me? Was it too much to ask? What if she did not love me? Did my love scare her, or hers for me?

I had been alone too long.

'Robert, please hold my hand again, like you did yesterday.' Her voice was anxious, wavering. She clearly too had not slept the night before.

Helena began to speak.

'Robert, I am flawed, perhaps too flawed. All my life I have been living in a box; a box without holes or light, a box with four sides, a floor and a lid, the corners always in the same place. Everything is totally organised within that box, never out of place. I respond to noise signals. I am like a rat, a rat that scientist, what was his name, Pavlov, yes Pavlov trained. I am trained to react to stimuli that exclude light, that exclude sight. Alarms, bells, whistles, furniture in the same place; nothing ever out of order.

Because I am blind, my emotions and longings have had to be in the same order. I've never had a boyfriend, never been with a man, only ever hugged by my mother or by a friend like Marge. I've never had a date or been to a dance. Nobody, not even my mother, has seen me without my glasses for nearly twenty years.

All my life has been spent here, really nowhere, a small town with fewer and fewer white people, not that it makes much difference to me. It's just the community in which I live.'

'Don't you think I've thought of that?' I questioned softly, almost breathless, my heart pounding.

'I know you have, I trusted you from the moment I heard your voice. I trust you because Marge and Jim call you their friend. When they speak of you it is more than that. How you helped them when they lost Adam. How they look forward to your visits. I feel safe with you when we walk in the veld, I want you to teach me to swim. I've always wanted to swim.' She faltered for a moment.

'But in one way I am lucky. I've been able to develop one emotion above all others and that is love. I can't be jealous or envy what others have, in terms of possessions or education, looks or anything else, as I never have been able to see it, let alone visualise it. I've never had to be very cross, angry, always been protected. Black and white; racial issues mean nothing to me. The black people here are as protective of me as the white people, perhaps even more so. I know nothing of politics, and religious issues pass me by. My mother is like a quiet Buddhist, so tolerance and forgiveness is the same as love.'

'Helena, what are you saying to me?'

And then she smiled, a glorious open smile, a smile so innocent and yet so exciting.

'Take my glasses off Robert, kiss me. I will be your girl.'

***

Yesterday, in our garden on a resplendent summer's afternoon we celebrated our 25th wedding anniversary.

Surrounded by our friends, some of them blind or partially sighted, guide dogs all around. Her mother, who is now very frail, and our two children both adults were there, our son an officer candidate in the Armed Forces, our daughter a computer programmer. Helena is still the beautiful woman I fell in love with and married. She carries her beauty, inner and outer, without sensing it. Everyone just adores her.

Canada has been good for her. We settled in a small town which has a school for the blind. From the time we arrived she has been the piano teacher there. Every so often we motor to the surrounding towns and she tunes the instruments belonging to clients, all of whom are her friends.

Our lives and home are governed by order and timetables. It has to be like this, for her to cope. But the spontaneity is there. Her lovemaking is intense, at times ferocious. She exercises with me every day. Music is always playing. I look at this beautiful woman who had faith in me to move into a different world, out of her box. My love for her is beyond belief.

We still return to Africa, not as often as I did in the past - every second or third year now. Much has changed, but Marge and Jim are still on the farm; their two sons run it and they have bought the adjacent one as well. Adam's little grave is carefully tended, we always spend some time there. I have never told Helena the full story, how Marge and I knew that Adam was our son. There is always a secret to be kept.

★★★